HER WINNING FORMULA

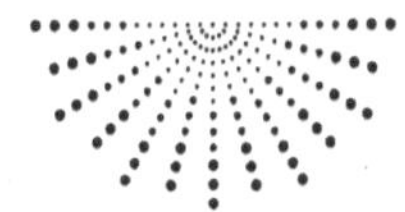

SHANNYN SCHROEDER

Originally Published: November 2014

ISBN: 978-1-950640-10-2

CONTENTS

Felicity Stone eased her way past the crowd hovering by the boarding gate. God, how she hated airports. Most people were afraid of flying or crashing. For her, being crammed with over a hundred other people was torture. She sought out the farthest seat she could find while she waited for the announcement to board.

It had been bad enough that she had to switch planes, in Chicago of all places, but her first flight had been delayed. Her original thought when she found she had a connecting flight in Chicago was to convince her friend Charlie to meet her at O'Hare for lunch. Then, with any luck, she'd be able to convince Charlie she needed to go on spring break vacation even if it meant letting Felicity buy her plane ticket. The plane being late ruined that plan.

She huffed out her irritation and set her hefty backpack on the floor at her feet. She checked her phone and saw the text from Layla. Her car had broken down in Georgia. Felicity jumped from her seat. Another text said that her wallet had been stolen and included the license and picture of some guy that Layla had decided to go home with. *What the heck was she thinking?* Layla had always been too quick to trust. At least she left a trail of proof of who this guy was.

Felicity dialed Layla's number and paced. She'd barely gotten three feet when someone tapped her shoulder. She turned and looked up and up. The guy was probably about six feet tall, towering over her barely-over-five-foot height, and had dark scruff covering his jaw. She widened her eyes in expectation of the reason for his interruption.

He lifted her bag from his side. "I think you left this—"

She blew out a breath and disconnected the call. "So what? I'm trying to make a call."

"The thing is, we're in an airport, and I really can't afford not to get to Texas on time."

"I don't control the plane."

"But a bag left unattended might get reported." He still had her bag, dangling from his fingers as though it weighed a few ounces.

"You're being a bit paranoid, don't you think? Every bag left sitting doesn't contain a—"

His other hand quickly covered her mouth. "I will pay you twenty dollars to not finish that sentence. Department of Homeland Security and the TSA do not take kindly to that word being used in an airport."

She swiped his hand away from her and

snatched her bag from him. Swinging it over her shoulder, she felt the weight pull at her back.

The guy looked at her and smiled—seriously smiled—and then put out his hand. "I'm Lucas, by the way, and I'm normally not so paranoid, but I have a wedding to get to, and if this plane doesn't leave on time, my family might kill me."

"So are you going around policing all of the passengers, or just me?"

He dropped his hand and shrugged. "I noticed your bag and was afraid it might be a problem. Sorry I bothered you."

He turned and walked away, taking the seat two over from where she had staked out her spot. There were four other seats in that row. Did he have to sit within touching distance of her? Felicity took a deep breath. She knew her thoughts were slightly unreasonable. The stress was getting to her.

Layla was stuck in Georgia, but she'd be okay until Felicity landed and could get her some cash. Another deep breath. Layla would *not* leave her to attempt to do spring break on her own. She and Layla went to school mere miles from each other but hardly ever hung out. Their schedules were hectic, so Felicity was really looking forward to spring break. This would be their last spring break since they were all graduating, except Charlie who needed an extra year. By this time next year, Layla would be working at the NSA doing mysterious government security and Felicity would be working at her father's lab in the R & D department developing her own perfume. Frivolous vacations probably wouldn't happen.

Felicity walked back to her seat and wrestled her textbook from her bag. Working out equations would soothe her and ease the gnawing stress. She was scribbling furiously through an equation when she felt another tap on her shoulder. She glanced up and saw the guy staring at her again.

"They're boarding. You were pretty engrossed in what you were doing, so I wasn't sure if you heard."

She blinked rapidly to clear the numbers from her mind. He turned and walked away. She slammed her book closed, and in looking at her watch, realized that she had been working for more than twenty minutes. She watched the guy step into the boarding line. He probably thought she was crazy, or maybe stupid. She shoved her book back in her bag and got in line.

As if sensing her presence, the guy—what the hell was his name?—turned again and looked down at her. "Business or pleasure?"

Now that she really paid attention to him without irritation poking her, she realized he was cute. His dark hair was a little messy, but his blue-gray eyes somehow managed to be both inviting and piercing. "Huh?"

"Are you going to Texas for business or pleasure?" He'd slowed his rate of speech like he was speaking to someone without command of the English language.

"Pleasure. Spring break with a friend."

His gaze wandered down her body and back up to her face. "What school do you go to?"

"Harvard."

His mouth opened, he paused, and then did it a couple of more times. Now who looked like he didn't know English?

"South Padre Island?" he finally asked.

She nodded. The line shifted forward.

"You'll love it. It's a lot of fun."

The flight attendant at the gate asked for his boarding pass and welcomed him aboard. Felicity handed over hers as well, grateful to finally be getting on the plane. Not that she should be in a hurry now since Layla wouldn't be arriving for at least a few days. A sharp spear of panic hit her. What was she supposed to do alone for days?

Once on the plane, Felicity hooked right, suddenly aware that she was following the tall guy. She paused to make sure she was, in fact, in first class. The flight attendant looked at her pass and pointed toward her seat to confirm she was going the right way. As she walked down the aisle to her seat, Felicity saw the same darn guy in her spot. She absolutely couldn't catch a break today.

"Excuse me, you're in my seat."

He stood, checked his pass, and looked at the window seat beside him. He smiled at her again, this time flashing teeth and a dimple in his right cheek. Damn, he was cute. "Is there anyway you would consider switching with me? Even in first class, my legs are cramped. Being in the aisle allows me a little more space."

The smile dazzled her enough that it took a

minute to process what he was saying. She didn't want to give up her aisle seat. Taking the window seat effectively trapped her.

A little voice in her head said that there were worse things to be trapped by than a hot dude with a killer smile.

"Fine. Whatever." She stepped aside so he could move, and she slid into place by the window.

"Would you like me to put your bag up for you?"

"No. I'll keep it here." She smashed it under the seat as best she could. She would definitely need to be able to work some equations to get through this flight sitting next to him.

He took his seat. "Sorry, I didn't catch your name earlier."

She leveled a look at him. "I didn't give it."

His mouth slid into a half smile, enough to let the dimple peek. "I think we got off on the wrong foot. Hi, I'm Lucas. May I ask your name?"

"Felicity."

"Nice to meet you, Felicity."

She buckled her seat belt and willed the pilot to get moving.

"So, Harvard, huh? Where are you originally from?"

"Chicago."

"I'm from Chicago too. Small world. What's your major?"

"Chemistry." Even as she answered him, she knew he was trying to carry on a conversation and she should do more, but she wasn't any good at it.

The flight attendant did her usual safety speech, and the pilot announced they were ready for takeoff. Lucas buckled himself in and suddenly got quiet. The plane began to move, and Felicity felt the waves of tension coming from her seatmate. She looked at him from the corner of her eye. He had a death grip on the armrest, his knuckles white.

"Are you okay?"

He nodded.

She turned back to look out the window.

"Actually, no, I'm not. I don't like to fly."

"It's no big deal. The flight will only be a few hours."

"The takeoff and landing are what get to me. My kids have a habit of rattling off statistics, and one of them told me that almost thirty percent of crashes occur during that time."

"Kids?"

"I'm a teacher."

She studied him. She'd never had a teacher who looked like him. "Gym?"

"Special ed."

That surprised her. She couldn't imagine him in a room full of rowdy, out of control kids or kids who had a hard time learning. Gym teacher she could picture. He looked like the athletic type.

"I'm also the baseball coach. Which is why I didn't want to come on this trip. I had to leave my assistant coach in charge of practice while I'm gone."

She couldn't believe he was nervous. He continued to carry the conversation effortlessly. "Whose wedding?"

"My brother's. He met his fiancée in South Padre, and they decided to have a destination wedding. And of course, it had to be over spring break."

"I guess you didn't have a choice to skip it since it's your brother."

He laughed. The warm, rich sound tickled through her, and she couldn't help but smile back.

A small ping let them know they could release their seat belts, so Felicity did. "Takeoff is done," she whispered.

LUCAS TANNER'S LUNGS STOPPED WORKING AT THE sight of Felicity's smile. It felt like being hit by a line drive to the solar plexus. Her whole face transformed when she smiled. She had been cute before, but now she was beautiful. Her words finally registered in his head. They were flying smoothly. Takeoff had been uneventful. "Thank you," he said.

But she was already rummaging below her seat for her bag, paying no attention to him. "For what?"

So she was paying attention. "You kept me preoccupied with talking, and I didn't notice takeoff."

She didn't respond, just opened up a massive

textbook and began scribbling in a notebook. He watched over her shoulder and couldn't figure out what the hell she was working on. An equation of some sort.

He was far from being stupid. Numbers didn't scare him, but the complex mess Felicity wrangled boggled his brain. Weird that she would be working while on break. Judging by the weight of her bag, she had other textbooks as well.

"What class is that?"

"Experimental synthetic chemistry," she answered without looking up.

"Why chemistry?"

"Why not? I like it. And my father is a chemist, so I'm guaranteed a job after graduation."

He'd never met a woman who gave such short answers lacking in detail. "Can I buy you a drink?"

This caught her attention, and she faced him. "You don't have to pay for drinks."

"I know. I wanted to get your attention. You were doing a good job of responding instead of ignoring me, the way most of my students would, but you weren't very invested in the conversation." He reached over, his hand brushing hers in the process, and ran a finger over the equation she'd been working on. "You're on vacation. You're supposed to be enjoying yourself."

She shifted uncomfortably and laid her palm over the work. "I enjoy chemistry."

"Is that really work you need to do now? If it is, I'll leave you alone." He waited for a reaction. She stared at him. "Tell me about yourself."

"What do you want to know?" She eased the cover closed on the book.

"Who are you meeting in Texas?"

"I'm supposed to be meeting my friend Layla, but her car broke down in Georgia. She has to wait to get it fixed."

A beautiful, smart girl who was alone for at least a few days. What more could he ask for? Showing up with a sexy woman on his arm should definitely dissuade Becky from thinking he'd be interested in a repeat.

"I'm sorry to hear about your friend. Do you have stuff planned to keep you busy while you're waiting for her?"

Felicity shook her head.

He leaned a little closer and caught her scent, something unique, not overly fruity or flowery, but it drew him in, making him want to bury his nose in her neck. "What perfume are you wearing?"

"Something I made."

"You make your own perfume?"

She smiled again. "Chemistry major. I can create all kinds of fabulous things."

"How?"

"My dad let me play around a lot as a kid. It's all about finding the right mix of fragrance in the right amounts." She held out her wrist. "For instance, this has a base note, or scent, of jasmine, and then I added middle notes of lavender and ylang-ylang."

He held her wrist, rubbed his fingers over the

pulse, and then lowered his nose to sniff. "Beauti-ful," he whispered across her skin.

She carefully extracted her arm from his grasp.

He offered her his best let's-get-to-know-each-other smile. "I have a proposition for you."

"Excuse me?"

"Nothing indecent. How would you like to go to the wedding as my date?"

She pulled back so quickly, she almost smacked her head on the window. "I wouldn't."

Maybe he'd misinterpreted her signals. They'd been weak, but he thought she was interested. After all, she'd abandoned chemistry for a conversation with him. "Do you have a boyfriend? If so, I wasn't implying it would have to be more than a friendly date."

"No boyfriend."

Hmm...her reaction to a simple invitation struck him as odd. "Do you have some aversion to weddings or me?"

"Weddings. Definitely weddings." Her eyes widened as she spoke.

It wasn't much, but he'd take the ego boost. "Why?"

"There are so many people, and they want to hug you and crowd your space." Then she added an eye roll. "And the ridiculous dancing."

"Well, no one would hug you at this wedding because they don't know you, and I won't make you perform the chicken dance."

Her brow furrowed in confusion. "You're a good-looking guy. Why me? There are probably a hundred single women on this plane, at least ten right here in first class."

"The truth is, Felicity, you're pretty, and I've enjoyed talking to you. Anyone who can make me forget takeoff is special. I'd like you to be my date because the maid of honor is my ex."

"So you want to make her jealous?"

"God, no. I want her to stay away from me. My soon to be sister-in-law keeps dropping hints that Becky is available if I want a second shot, which I don't."

Felicity held her closed textbook in a tight grip, looking eerily similar to how he'd held on during takeoff.

"You just said your friend is delayed and you have no other plans. Sitting in your hotel room alone isn't much of a spring break."

She bit her lower lip. "I don't think so, but thanks for the invitation."

With that, she flopped the cover back on her book and began working.

His determination kicked in. He knew neither of them would find a better deal. "What would it take for you to agree?"

She didn't look up from her book. "What are you offering?"

"Free dinner."

She glanced out of the corner of her eye. "Wedding food is always crap."

"You get to drink for free."

"Not much of a drinker."

"What do you want then?"

She shrugged.

He checked his watch. By his estimation, he had another couple of hours sitting beside her. During that time he might come up with the right incentive to interest Felicity. He let her work on her equations while he checked his phone.

Without looking up from her work, Felicity said, "For someone who was worried about my unattended bag, you're quick to break the rules to try to use your phone."

He smiled and held the phone for her to see. "It's in airplane mode. I have an app for texting. Still following the rules."

Returning his attention to the phone, he saw he had at least twelve texts, not surprising since his family had expected him on an earlier flight. Obviously, none of them had bothered to listen to the voice mail messages he'd left. His original flight had offered him a free ticket if he agreed to be bumped. Although he had no plans for another vacation, one look at the desperate woman who really wanted to be on that plane, and he'd agreed.

The next flight, this one, had been delayed because of a late connection, which led him to Felicity. And his students thought karma didn't exist. He shot off texts to everyone, letting them know he was in the air and would make it in time for rehearsal. Now all he had to do was convince Felicity to be his date.

CHAPTER TWO

Felicity felt Lucas's eyes on her, even when he wasn't looking in her direction. He'd made some excellent points. What was she going to do while waiting for Layla? It would probably only be a couple of days, but still. This was supposed to be vacation—their last spring break to celebrate Layla's awesome job offer. Felicity could handle a couple of days by herself. It would be like most of her weekends.

She looked down at the equation she'd been working on and realized that she'd taken a wrong turn. She didn't do that. Distractions didn't affect her. At least not normally. Something about Lucas made her want to close the text again and put down her pencil. She remembered the way he'd pointed at her work and brushed his hand across hers in the process. The accidental touch had caused warmth to spread slowly up her arm.

Lucas had finally given up on trying to get her into a conversation, so she refocused on the page in front of her. She'd had to erase the last few lines of work and backtrack to find her error. Sitting next to a guy shouldn't do this to her. He'd done nothing more than talk. She was surrounded by guys all the time in just about every class she had. Not too many of them were as sexy as Lucas though.

She stole a look at him. He sat sprawled in the seat, his long legs extending into the aisle, and he had to shift every time someone wanted to get by. And for each person, he added a polite, "I'm sorry," as he moved his legs out of the path. Even though he was in the middle of texting furiously on his phone, his smile was at the ready. It was like each passerby couldn't help but return the smile.

He put in earbuds, and Felicity heard the harsh beat of heavy metal. A few minutes later, it was something thumpy like rap. Checking her watch, she knew they should be landing soon, so she packed up her stuff and closed her eyes to relax. The pilot came on and asked everyone to take their seats and fasten their seat belts because they might hit a bit of turbulence.

Felicity followed the directions and checked Lucas. He didn't seem to hear the pilot, but his seat belt had never been loosened. The plane hit a quick bump, and Lucas ripped his earbuds out. "What the hell was that?"

"Just a little turbulence. Nothing to worry about."

His hands grasped the armrest in the death grip again. Felicity reached over and picked up one of the abandoned earbuds and held it to her ear. "You listen to Pink?"

Lucas's eyes were shut tight, but he nodded. "I listen to what my students listen to. Gives me insight."

"They listen to Metallica?"

"No, that was for me."

They hit another pocket of turbulence, this time with enough force to shake things around them. Lucas looked like he was in pain. She laid her hand over his on the armrest. "It'll be okay. We're not going to crash. It's a wind current going against everything else."

He flipped his hand over and held hers, but didn't open his eyes. Warmth spread up her arm at his touch. She had no idea what else to say. There truly wasn't anything to be afraid of. She'd flown plenty over the years and turbulence happened. She remembered that talking had helped distract him and relax him during takeoff. Unfortunately for him, she sucked at conversation.

"So why are you trolling the airplane for a date instead of bringing a girlfriend to the wedding?"

He peeked from his squinted eyelids. "I don't have a girlfriend. I've instituted a moratorium on dating."

She snickered. He willingly placed his dating life on hold, and she didn't know how to get a date. "Why?"

"Long story. Anyway, I saw you and I figured, why not? I'm not looking to start a relationship. I only need to get through the wedding and you're on spring break."

His face was more relaxed now, and the only sign of his discomfort was his hand linked with hers. But even that was pleasant.

He smiled. "You must think I'm the biggest wuss on the planet."

"No. We all have our hang-ups. Lucky for you, I'm good at flying."

"My brother thought it would be better in first class. He was wrong."

"Everything is better in first class."

The pilot announced their descent, and Lucas inhaled sharply and closed his eyes, but didn't release her hand. She wasn't even sure if he was aware he held it. The wheels touched down with little more than a bump, and Felicity nudged him. "It's over."

"Thanks." He finally let go of her.

She missed the warmth of his hand the moment it was gone. "Well, good luck with the wedding."

"Can I have your number? Maybe we can get together for a drink or something this week."

"I thought you were on a dating break."

"I didn't give up drinking with friends. After being stuck next to me while I was in a panic, I think I can call you a friend."

She thought for a moment, and then stopped herself. What was there to consider? If he called and she changed her mind, she didn't have to answer. She pulled out her phone and asked for his number and called him so he'd have hers.

Felicity followed Lucas off the plane and to baggage claim, where he kindly lifted her bag from the carousel for her. Then she ended up following him to the car rental counter. One attendant took his name and looked up his reservation. "Your car will be pulled around in a few minutes."

The other clerk asked her to spell her name three times. "Are you sure you booked with us, miss? I'm not showing any reservation."

"Yes, I'm sure." At least pretty sure. "Just book me something now then."

"I can't. We're out of cars. It is spring break. Can I call you a taxi?" The girl's sweet southern drawl couldn't even cover the sting of information.

Felicity was beginning to think this trip was cursed.

Lucas stood there staring at her, then he sighed. "Take my car. I can have someone from my family come get me."

"I can't do that."

"Sure you can. I'm probably going to be at the hotel most of the time." He leaned over the counter and flashed a sexy smile at the clerk. "You can change that reservation, right? I'd like to give my friend Felicity here my car."

The girl's face brightened. "Of course, we can do that."

Felicity pulled out her credit card. "Thank you."

Lucas had stepped away from the counter and pulled out his phone. She watched him and knew she should do or say something. *Thank you* didn't quite cut it. She thought about Layla and Charlie and even her mother and what they would do in this situation. "Don't call your family. I'll take you to your hotel."

"You sure?"

"It doesn't make sense for someone to drive thirty miles to get here and then have to turn back. It's the least I can do." She signed the paperwork, and they walked outside to get the car. Felicity slid her sunglasses on her face as Lucas stowed their bags in the trunk. He climbed in beside her, looking no more comfortable than he had on the plane. "I'm a safe driver."

He jiggled the handle to adjust the seat and shoved it back to allow more legroom, and then he relaxed. He typed his hotel information into the onboard GPS, and Felicity began driving. Lucas made call after call while they drove. From what she could hear, he'd been roped into taking care of a bunch of wedding details, but nothing seemed to bother him.

When he finally clicked his phone off and tucked it back in his pocket, she knew she should say something.

"Sorry for all the calls. My family was a little panicked that I wasn't going to make it on time."

"Okay." In the silence, she thought about what she'd wanted to get out of this vacation, besides time with her two closest and oldest friends. She wanted to have fun. She'd been counting on Layla and Charlie to help with that. It was bad enough that Charlie refused the trip, but now Layla was late. As they neared Lucas's hotel, she blurted, "Okay, I'll go to the wedding with you."

"You make it sound like it might be torture."

She laughed. "After you see me in a big crowd, you might think that way too."

"It'll be fun."

Ha! Volunteering to put herself into a group of people she didn't know didn't sound fun at all, but being with Lucas did. He made her laugh, which was something she didn't get from most guys.

LUCAS RELAXED HIS SHOULDERS. HE HAD A DATE for the wedding. This would be perfect. Felicity would be able to keep Becky from clawing at him, and he might actually have a shot of enjoying this week.

Felicity pulled up in front of his hotel. "Give me a call and let me know what time I should be here tomorrow."

"Tomorrow? No, I need you now."

Her eyes widened, and he realized how his words sounded. "I mean, there's rehearsal in a couple of hours and then dinner after. My family will expect my date to be there. Plus, you'll need a crash course on me and my family if we're going to pull this off."

Felicity's brows furrowed, and a cute wrinkle waved along her forehead. "Pull this off? I thought you just needed a date."

He released a slow breath. "I need a date to

keep my ex away. If she knows we just met on the plane, it'll be like waving a red cape at a bull. She needs to think we're in a relationship."

Felicity swallowed hard.

"We don't need to make them believe we're getting married or anything, just dating, but that means we need to know about each other."

"But...but I have to check in at my hotel."

"Call and tell them you'll be late. You can go there after dinner tonight." Lucas waited patiently, like he did in the classroom when a student needed time to develop an answer.

Felicity faced forward, staring out the windshield, looking like she was carrying on a conversation in her head. She blew out a breath and shook her head. "Fine. Get the bags from the trunk and I'll park. I need to change before dinner."

"Thanks. I could kiss you."

She turned, and one eyebrow arched up above her sunglasses. "Is that part of our deal?"

He smiled. "Only if you want it to be."

He waited a beat for her reaction, but she offered none. He climbed from the car, pulled their suitcases out, and waited for her at the curb. They would need a cover story about how they met and how long they'd been dating. The fact that Felicity seemed to be a quiet person would work in her favor; his family loved to talk.

Walking back toward the front door, Felicity looked younger than she was. Her backpack was slung over one shoulder, and she kept her eyes down, shielded from everything. He bent over, grabbed both bags, and followed Felicity into the lobby. He checked in and got her a room key in case he had to go deal with some family crisis before the rehearsal, which was likely to happen. If he let her go to her hotel, she might not come back. She looked more spooked than he'd been on the plane.

In the elevator, she said, "So what do I need to know?"

"It's my older brother, Andy, getting married to Kelly. Kelly's best friend is Becky, my ex. Unfortunately, since I'm best man, I have to spend some time with her, but I decided to show up later than everyone else to limit that engagement. I also have a younger sister, Mia. She's a sophomore at Northwestern."

"Do I get a cheat sheet for this?"

"You won't need one. My family is really friendly. The wedding isn't going to be too big. Most of my extended family isn't making the trip, so the guests are mostly friends, and they won't care if you can remember names. They'll be too busy dancing and drinking." They stepped off the elevator and he started speed walking down the hall.

"In a hurry?" Her short legs had a hard time keeping up.

"The wedding party has a block of rooms here. If we don't hurry, someone will come out and see us before we're ready." He dropped the bags with a thump at the door and slid the key card in. He held the door open for Felicity and followed.

She walked slowly through the room and settled at a chair by the window.

"Your turn," he said.

"I'm an only child."

"And?"

"And what? I live with my parents when I'm not at school. My dad owns a cosmetics company, and after graduation, I'll work for him." She sat, straight-backed like she was reciting a story.

"Relax. I'm just trying to get to know you. What's your favorite color? What do you do in your free time? Tell me about your friends." He sat on the corner of the bed closest to her and leaned his elbows on his knees.

She studied her hands in her lap. "I make my own perfume. But you already know that. I don't have a favorite color. Maybe blue? I own a lot of blue, so it would make it my favorite, right?"

"Tell me about Layla."

Felicity looked up with a smile on her face. "You'd love Layla. And Charlie—Charlotte. We've been friends since high school. Layla's a math geek at MIT, and she was just offered a job at the NSA. That was the whole purpose of our trip. To celebrate. Charlie...Charlie's fun. She's into video games and computers. She never left Chicago, though." She paused and closed her eyes. "I really wish they were here."

He felt bad for her. The only time she looked at ease was when she spoke about her friends. He wished they were here for her too. He reached out and touched her hand. "So, science, math, and computers. Did you guys form your own nerd club?"

She opened her eyes and smiled again, but kicked his shin. "We'd make one kick-ass nerd club."

"Is that how you all met?"

"In a nerd club? No. We actually all had English together as freshmen. We just clicked. Which, in case you're really dense, isn't something that happens easily for me." Her smile didn't quite make it to her eyes.

There, he still saw fear, but she hadn't brushed his hand away. "We clicked."

"But you're easy."

He jerked back exaggeratedly. "Should I be offended?"

She covered her face. "That's not what I meant. See, this is never going to work. I do things like that all the time. You'd be better off taking your chances with Becky."

"I was kidding. You'll be fine." He thought for a moment. She was a science major, who liked formulas. The idea struck. "What if I give you a plan, a step-by-step plan, to get you through the wedding?"

"What?"

"You like science. I'm guessing you like the answers, knowing things have to work out. The rules of it. I'll give you the rules."

She looked thoughtful for a minute, almost like she planned to argue. "So give me rules."

He stood and paced the room. "Rule one:

When someone asks a question, keep your answer simple, but detailed."

"At the risk of sounding stupid, I need explanation." She shifted and pulled one leg under her in the chair.

"If someone asks who you are, you don't just say 'Felicity.' You answer, 'I'm Felicity. I came with Lucas, the groom's brother.' This gives the person enough to ask a follow-up question and keeps you from sounding rude."

She opened her mouth and then snapped it shut without comment.

"That leads us to rule two: If they don't ask a follow-up question, you should. Ask something simple. Think in terms of 'And you?' So if I ask how you're doing, you answer and then say, 'And you?'"

Felicity stood in front of him. "I'm Felicity. I came with Lucas, the groom's brother. And you?" She narrowed her eyes. "I sound stupid."

"I said think in terms of 'And you,' not that you should only use those words. You're at a wedding. You can ask which side of the party they're there for, bride or groom. You can ask where they're from, what they do for a living." He began to feel like maybe he was crazy for attempting this. She would never be able to sell this to Becky.

"Wait. That's it." She pushed past him and went to the nightstand. Grabbing a pen and pad of paper, she said, "Give me a list of appropriate questions. I can memorize anything in record time."

Lucas crossed his arms, not sure how a list would help.

"I may be socially inept, but I can figure out not to ask someone what they do for a living when they've asked where I go to school. It'll be like my own multiple choice test in my head."

She stepped closer, and the scent of her perfume grabbed him again.

"I can do this," she whispered.

He wondered if she was trying to convince him or herself.

CHAPTER THREE

Armed with a list of appropriate questions for small talk with family and the bridal party, as well as mental images of Lucas's immediate family, Felicity rode the elevator down to meet up with Lucas at the rehearsal. She tried to convince him that she didn't need to be there for the rehearsal and showing up for dinner would be enough to convince everyone that she existed, but once his mother heard that he'd brought a date, she insisted that Felicity join them for the actual rehearsal on the beach.

She walked through the lobby and out the back entrance of the hotel, which led to the beach. Nerves fluttered in her stomach, but she swallowed hard and ignored them. After a few steps into the sand, she stopped and removed her sandals. Whoever thought dress shoes and the beach mixed was sorely mistaken. A crowd gathered near the water, but not so close that they'd get wet.

At the edge of the circle of people, she waited

patiently, having no idea what she was supposed to do. Lucas looked over his shoulder. His gaze met hers and he smiled. Something warm tumbled in her chest, and she looked behind her to see who that smile was meant for because surely it wasn't her. But she was alone. He winked and her nerves fled.

Even while he watched her, he carried on a conversation with the bride and his mother. Whatever it was, they were serious, and as Lucas spoke, Felicity could almost see the tension dissipate. People lined up and walked, and shuffled around as directed by the reverend.

Felicity always thought of wedding ceremonies as quiet affairs, but not with Lucas's family. Their voices carried over the waves and children playing nearby. It was like yelling was their normal mode of communication. She followed Lucas's every move, his presence keeping her calm, even though he only spared a glance in her direction every now and then, like he needed to make sure she was still there.

As the group started the second trial run, a girl moved to stand beside Felicity. Felicity scanned her memory. This had to be Mia, the younger sister.

"Hi, you must be Felicity, Lucas's date."

"I am. And you're Mia, right?"

The girl nodded, her dark hair blowing in the breeze. She had the same blue, friendly eyes Lucas had, and her smile was every bit as engaging.

"Lucas told me you go to Northwestern, but

he didn't say what you're studying." So it was more of an observation than a question, but it worked. *Yay, Felicity!*

"English. I want to teach or maybe write. I haven't decided yet." She tilted her head and studied Felicity's face. "Harvard, huh? What are you doing slumming with my brother?"

"Slumming?"

Mia smiled. "It's a joke. Kind of. He's not exactly Ivy League material."

He was better than most Ivy League guys that Felicity had hung out with. Felicity didn't have a follow-up question for that. She didn't know what to say, so she shrugged. Mia plopped down in the sand, so Felicity figured the conversation was over.

No one else seemed to take notice of her, so she stepped away from the crowd to call Layla. As the phone rang, she dug her toes into the sand, hot on top, cool beneath. It was the opposite of how she usually felt.

"Hey, Felicity, hang on a minute."

Although Layla covered the mouthpiece, Felicity could hear her having a conversation with a guy. Probably the one she'd sent a picture of.

"Hi. Thanks for getting back to me so quickly."

Layla's voice held an unusual quality. "Hey, Layla, are you okay? What happened?"

"My car broke down. The transmission needs to be rebuilt. It's going to take a few days. Then as I was trying to drown my sorrows in a beer, someone stole my wallet. I have twenty bucks to my name." She paused. "Make that forty bucks."

For someone whose life just crashed, Layla didn't sound too upset. "Tell me what you need."

"I have a new credit card being sent. It'll be here Tuesday. In the meantime, I made a friend. His name is Phin. I sent you his picture. Did you get it?"

"Hell, yeah, I did. He's hot. Are you with him now?" Felicity tried not to be jealous. Layla hadn't even been trying to find a guy and she did. Made a friend, just like that.

"Yeah, he's here."

"Do you want me to book a hotel for you?"

"Uh, no, I'm gonna stay here. Phin has a spot for me."

There was more shifting on the line, and Layla sounded out of breath. "Are you sure you're okay? You sound funny."

"Yep. Great. Reeeeally great. I'll call you later, okay. Have fun."

Felicity finally put the pieces together. "Oh, you're getting busy right now, aren't you?"

Layla giggled. Yeah, she'd made some friend all right.

"Jeez, that's just wrong. Call me later." Felicity disconnected and rolled her eyes. When she turned around, she crashed into Lucas.

"Hey, everything okay?"

Felicity shook her head. "My friend's car broke down, and it's the transmission. She's stuck in Georgia for at least a few days."

The reality of that hit her. She was going to

spend half her vacation alone. "But she made a friend. So while she's off having fun with some guy, I'm stuck here alone at a wedding full of people I've never met."

Lucas put his arm around her like it was the most natural thing. "You're not alone, babe. You're with me."

So, she had something to do with a bunch strangers for today and tomorrow. What then? She supposed she could sit on the beach and read. Her e-reader was packed with juicy books, things that would take her brain far from formulas and equations. Lucas led her back to the group and introduced her to everyone he'd told her about earlier and then some.

Mostly, she kept her mouth shut unless someone asked a direct question, but Lucas's ex kept throwing some glares in her direction. Part of Felicity had believed that Lucas was a little full of himself to think that his ex wanted another chance. Didn't every guy believe that? But judging by the looks Felicity was getting, he'd been right. Becky was upset that he'd brought a date.

As a group, they went to the restaurant. There was one big table for the bridal party, and Felicity's stomach churned. Lucas made her come to this, and he was going to abandon her. She stiffened every muscle to prevent shaking.

"Hey, Mom. I'm going to sit over here with Felicity."

"Sure, honey. I understand." She paused, looked at the large table, and then added, "Unless you'd like to join us, Felicity?"

Felicity flinched, but she didn't think anyone else noticed. Lucas looked down at her and said, "No. We'll take a table over here."

His mother nodded, her short ponytail swinging behind her head. Lucas turned them toward a table in the corner. It wasn't until they sat that she released a pent-up breath. "Thank you for that. I wouldn't have done well at such a large table."

Lucas reached across the table and touched her hand. "You're doing fine. Mia likes you."

"We spoke about ten words to each other."

"It was enough." He shrugged and opened the menu. "Order whatever you want."

Felicity watched him. He didn't let go of her hand although no one else was paying attention. How real did he expect this fake relationship to be? With her free hand, she opened her menu and stared at the choices. There was a lot of seafood. Yuck.

She leaned forward and whispered, "Would it be really bad if I ordered a burger? I'm kind of a picky eater, and I don't see much that I like."

Lucas looked up from his menu. "Order whatever you want."

"I don't want it to look bad if I'm supposed to order something fancy. I don't want your family to think you're dating some freak." Even though, in a way, it was totally true.

He reached out and tilted her chin toward the head table. "See that guy over there, the old one with gray hair? That's my dad. He's a plumber. His idea of fancy is ordering a steak and a loaded baked potato. No one will question your food choice."

His hand on her face did odd things to her stomach, much like thinking about being in a room of strangers, but not in a bad way. "What about Becky?"

"I don't care about Becky."

Felicity eased away from his reach. "You must care at least a little or you wouldn't have asked me to be here."

"I really don't. I just didn't want to cause a scene with her. My hope is that when she sees me with you, she'll realize that I'm really not interested and I've moved on."

"But you haven't."

"I have."

"Then why don't you have a real girlfriend here?"

"Shh! Lower your voice." He looked over his shoulder. "I told you I'm on a break from dating. But I have dated other girls since breaking up with Becky. I'm just not in a relationship right now."

The waiter arrived to take their order. Felicity's attention returned to the menu. "Can I get a hamburger, well done. Plain. Ketchup on the side."

"Fries with that?"

"Yes."

"Something to drink?"

"Just water."

"Can we have two glasses of white wine as well, please?" Lucas asked. When her eyes shot up, he patted her hand. "One glass won't kill you."

Then he ordered a steak with vegetables. While he spoke with the waiter, Felicity looked around the room, careful not to make eye contact with anyone. She'd learned early on in life that if she didn't want people to talk to her, all she had to do was avoid eye contact.

"Hey, Lucas, come here," the groom called from across the room.

Lucas stood. "Excuse me. I'll be right back."

But he wasn't. He went to the head table, engaged in conversation with his brother. Then he dealt with three other people who seemed to have complaints or problems in one form or another. The last person to tug his attention was Becky.

The woman was pretty, in a very conventional way. Her nails sparkled. Her glossy blond hair waved past her shoulders and shone when the light struck it. She could easily be the heroine from one of the romance novels Felicity read. Then Felicity imagined her being tied up and spanked and the picture no longer agreed with the package. She stifled a snort.

She continued to watch the interaction between Lucas and Becky, knowing she could learn from it. For all the money her parents had spent on her education, the one thing that she was lacking was the simplest. She didn't know how to act with people.

She'd known her whole life that she was different. In elementary school, everyone attributed it to her being smarter than her peers. In high school, she met Layla and Charlie, both of whom were every bit as intelligent. They befriended her despite her weirdness. But she realized that even among other intelligent people, she was different.

Layla and Charlie knew it too, and they helped her. She never would've gotten a boyfriend if it hadn't been for them. Relationships always started with being fixed up and then they would double or triple date until Felicity was comfortable with the guy. Until he got used to her quirks.

Which was why she really needed Layla this week. Lucas was doing a good job of getting her through the weekend, but then what? She couldn't expect him to follow her around all week.

Or could she? He said he owed her. Maybe this was how he could pay her back.

LUCAS HANDLED EVERY ISSUE THAT HAD COME HIS way from friends and family members. As he tried to get back to his table with Felicity, more people stopped him. He usually didn't mind the interruptions, but something about Felicity made him want to be at the table alone with her. Which definitely didn't bode well for his moratorium on women.

But Felicity was different. She wasn't just shy or introverted; in some ways, she reminded him of some of his students. Although she obviously didn't have a learning disability, she exhibited many of the same social deficits he dealt with on a daily basis. And she totally charmed him.

He'd planned to be here for only part of the week, but if he could convince Felicity to hang out with him, he might be persuaded to stay. He shook his head as he finally made his way back to the table. Another messed-up woman was not what his life needed right now.

As he reclaimed his seat across from Felicity, her eyes remained on him. He'd watched her all night, and she rarely made eye contact, but she'd tracked his every move. "Sorry about that."

"It's okay. I'd rather have you go off and address questions than force me to come with. I hate feeling like a tagalong."

He picked up his glass of wine. "To a convenient friendship." She stared at him, so he waved his glass again. "A toast."

Her eyes widened, and she brought her glass to his for a gentle clink. "To friendship?"

He shifted closer to her, wanting to catch a whiff of her perfume again. "Do you *not* want to be my friend?"

"I'm not sure. If we agree to be friends, won't that ruin the image you're trying to project?"

"We can be friends and still convince my family that we're more."

Her eyebrows came together over her brown eyes.

"Don't worry. I'm not talking about letting them catch us naked. Just a pose here or there." He leaned closer. "Like this. Sitting close like this gives an air of intimacy."

Her chest rose and fell rapidly. She hung on every word. He watched her mouth as her tongue darted out and moistened her lips. He wanted to feel those lips, taste them.

"Hey, Lucas, are you trying to avoid me?"

Felicity jolted back in her seat.

Instead of pulling away, Lucas scooted his chair closer to Felicity in order to face Becky. "No, Becky, I'm not avoiding you. I'm enjoying dinner with my date. Felicity, this is Becky, maid of honor."

Becky gave Felicity the once-over and extended her hand. "Nice to meet you."

Felicity shook hands, but said nothing. A predatory look came into Becky's eyes. Lucas knew that look. He'd been on the receiving end often enough during their brief relationship. He slid his arm around the back of Felicity's chair.

Although Felicity didn't lean into him the way most women would, his movement was enough to send a clear message to Becky. He hoped.

"I'd love to get to know you better. You two are staying here at the hotel, aren't you?"

"Of course," he answered, which earned him a swift kick from Felicity under the table.

Becky's brightly painted lips spread into a smile. "I have some maid of honor duties to attend to later in the day before the wedding, but I'd love to meet up for breakfast. Say about seven thirty? You are still an early riser, aren't you, Lucas?"

"We'll meet you then."

Becky spun on her high heels, dress swirling around her.

Felicity stared after her. "Why did you do that? There's no way I'm getting up early enough to get ready and come here for breakfast at seven thirty."

Shit. He'd completely forgotten that she planned to go to her own hotel after dinner. "So stay here. My room has two beds."

She looked at him from the corner of her eye, but gave no answer.

He moved her hair from her shoulder. The soft silkiness fell over his fingers. "Look, I wasn't thinking. Becky had a look on her face that told me she wanted to fuck with you, and I didn't want to give her reason. If she believes we're a couple, she'll leave you alone. I don't want you in an uncomfortable position just because you're my date."

"My life is an uncomfortable position." She pressed her lips together. "This vacation is supposed to be fun. I guess you're kind of fun. I'll stay."

"I guess I owe you again."

"You owe me more than a meal."

The waiter arrived with their dishes. Lucas slid away from her chair to allow them both room to maneuver. When the waiter left, Lucas asked, "You have ideas about how you want to be paid?"

She turned to look at him, and with a bright smile, she said, "I have a few ideas."

He really hoped her ideas and his coincided.

CHAPTER FOUR

After dinner and many conversations with people, Lucas pulled Felicity away from the crowd that had migrated to the nearest bar. She hadn't said anything, but her resolve to socialize had definitely wavered. She'd done exceptionally well with the questions he'd given her. She didn't stray far from them, so he knew she was running out of material.

He didn't know how she would handle tomorrow. They said their good-byes and headed to the elevator.

"Well, that was fun. Not." She sagged against the wall beside the elevator. "What the hell did I get myself into with you?"

The doors dinged and opened. She peeled herself away from the wall. He slid his hand against hers and interlaced their fingers. "You were pretty damn good. Thank you."

A blush rose in her cheeks. They stepped off the elevator, still holding hands. At his door, she let go. "I think the coast is clear."

Hmm...she thought he was holding her hand because they were being watched. It was a conversation best had inside the room. He swiped the key card and held the door open for her.

"Felicity, I was holding your hand because I wanted to. Not everything is because of an ulterior motive."

"Oh. Okay." She walked through the room, glanced at the beds, and grabbed her bag. "Which one do you want?"

He'd been hoping she might decide they should share a bed. "Doesn't matter."

"Then if it's all right with you, I'd prefer this one." She opened her suitcase on the bed and just stared at it for a moment. "Are you sure this is a good idea?"

"What?"

"All of this. Lying to your family. Pretending to be a couple. What happens when you go home? Won't Becky, and everyone else for that matter, be suspicious?"

"I don't see Becky on a regular basis. I just want to get through the wedding without her trying to rekindle anything with me. As an added bonus, I'm having fun with you."

"You are?"

"Yeah." Didn't anyone ever tell her that she was fun? He flopped on the bed. "So what do you want to do?"

"I'm going to read for a little bit." She closed her suitcase and set it on the floor on the far side of the bed. She pulled out an e-reader and scooted toward the headboard. She sat, legs extended, crossed at the ankle.

He settled back on his own bed. "Will the TV bother you?"

"No," she answered without looking up from her device.

Lucas flipped through channels and decided to rent an action movie. Not quite the action he'd been looking for, but it was better than hanging out with Andy and the rest of the bridal party. He kicked off his shoes and piled pillows behind him.

The movie was filled with killing and explosions, but couldn't hold his concentration. The mousy girl in the bed beside him kept grabbing his attention. And she wasn't doing anything but reading silently. She didn't even move her lips when she read, but her facial expressions changed. Her eyes would narrow or her forehead crinkled. Sometimes a sly smile snuck up on her. He didn't know how he knew, but it was like it surprised her when it happened.

He couldn't remember the last time he read anything for school that had him feeling any kind of emotion, much less what she was experiencing. He paused the movie. "What are you reading?"

She didn't look up from the book, but answered, "Research."

He tossed the remote on his bed and jumped onto her bed, jostling her in the process. "Come on. Research isn't that fascinating. What are you really reading?"

Annoyance crossed her face with his intrusion. "It is research. I enjoy research."

"Let me see." He held out his hand for the reader.

"No." She hugged it tight to her chest.

Now he had to know what it was. No one guarded research material. He crawled over to her, and she scooted farther back until she hit the headboard. "Let me see."

"No. Now go away and watch your movie."

"This is more interesting than the movie." He eyed the way she held it to figure out the best way to snatch the device.

She turned to get out of bed, presumably to get away from him, giving him his opening to grab the reader. He moved fast, and she stood looking in disbelief. Her mouth hung open and fear entered her eyes, but she covered it quickly with anger as she crossed her arms.

He hadn't yet looked down at the screen. "I'm just playing. If you really don't want me to see this, I'll stop."

"Whatever. Do what you want." She knelt on the bed and then sat, pulling her knees up to her chest. She bit her thumbnail.

He glanced down at the screen and began reading. He smiled. Felicity was reading a naughty book. "You're reading porn?"

"It's not porn. It's erotica or erotic romance."

"Chick porn."

"You're such a guy." She grabbed her reader back and turned away from him.

"Why did you call it research? Why not say you're reading a novel?"

"I *am* doing research."

"Sex research?"

She looked over her shoulder and rolled her eyes.

"You don't know...I mean...."

"Shut up, Lucas. I know how sex works. I've even had sex."

"Then why research?"

She huffed and put the reader down on the bed. "These books aren't just about the sex. They're about human interaction, relationships. How people relate to each other and learn to understand each other."

"That's just part of life."

"For people like you it is, not for me."

"For people like me?"

"I've known you for less than a day, but I can tell that everyone likes you. You're open and friendly, and you understand what people mean and what they need. I don't. I don't get any of that. I read these books because I get a picture of what normal people think when they see someone, how they interpret someone's words or actions."

He stared at her. He didn't know what to say. During the course of speaking, she opened up. Her body language relaxed, and she was in the moment, not worrying about anything. She was honest and vulnerable. It was pretty fucking sexy. He lay down and rested on his elbow. "Does it turn you on?"

She rolled her eyes again. "Such a guy."

She turned over on her stomach and went

back to reading. He mimicked her pose and bumped his shoulder into hers. "You didn't answer the question."

"Sometimes," she whispered.

The thought made his dick hard, and part of him was glad she wasn't looking at him. He knew she wasn't flirting or coming on to him; she was just being honest. He rested his head on his forearms on the bed. "Want to watch a movie with me? We could call it research too."

She waited a beat and then turned her head. "Are you making fun of me?"

"No. I'm trying to interact with you. I'd like to sit here and watch a movie together. I'll even let you pick. But no porn. I'm not that kind of guy."

Her eyes widened, and he knew she didn't get his joke. "I'm kidding, Felicity. Most guys aren't offended by porn."

"Okay. I don't think I want to watch porn anyway."

"We could call it research." He winked at her.

She rolled her eyes again. "I'm gonna take a shower."

"I'll finish this movie. You are going to come back and watch one with me, right?"

She stood beside the bed, digging through her suitcase before she smiled. "Sure."

From his position on the bed, he watched her walk into the bathroom, and he waited until she turned the water on. He pressed play on the movie, but his attention returned to the book Felicity was reading.

So much about the girl fascinated him. He couldn't afford to think like that. His fascination and need to rescue people was what caused all his trouble. He'd befriend Felicity and that would be it.

FELICITY STARTED THE WATER FOR THE SHOWER and stared at her reflection. She couldn't believe that she admitted all of that to Lucas. She'd never spoken that openly to anyone, except for Layla and Charlie, and even then, she didn't have to explain. They just got it.

She half expected him to laugh at her, but he didn't. He teased her, but she could tell he was just trying to make her laugh. After taking out her contacts, she stepped under the spray of the shower and relaxed. As the warm water eased her muscles, her mind wandered back to the book she'd been reading when Lucas had interrupted. The characters were making out, and Felicity had in fact been getting turned on.

She began to imagine Lucas doing what the character had done, tugging at her nipples with his teeth while his fingers gently rubbed her clit. Felicity mimicked the motions with her hands. The pleasure made her lean back against the cold tile wall, but she didn't stop. She plucked her nipple, first on one breast then the other as her other hand became slick. As she picked up the pace, her hips rocked against her hand.

Her head lolled back and she closed her eyes. She plunged two fingers inside herself. With her other hand, she rubbed and flicked at her clit. The tension built and coiled low in her stomach, and she moved faster, seeking release. When she came, she almost lost balance and slid around on the slick surface of the tub.

Water sluiced over her as she braced a hand against the wall. Her muscles relaxed and her nerves jumped. A moment passed, and then she heard Charlie's question from yesterday morning. *"When was the last time you had an orgasm with someone other than yourself?"*

As she washed her hair and then her body, Felicity answered honestly, "Too damn long." Lucas was on the other side of the door. What would he do if she just walked out there naked and wanted to have sex with him? He'd been flirting with her—at least she thought so. Given how often she misread signals, who knew? But then he said he only wanted her to pretend to be his date. Regardless of how he acted, his words were specific.

Plus, if he rejected the whole idea, his entire plan for the wedding would be ruined. She couldn't do that to him. He was a nice guy who gave up his rental car for her. And he'd given her a valuable lesson on social interaction. Lucas was excellent at social interaction. She could learn a lot from him. She turned off the water and stepped from the shower, determined to use Lucas as a mentor. She'd learn what she could and then use it for the rest of her trip.

She dried quickly, pulled on shorts and a shirt, and hoped she hadn't been in there too long. Slipping her glasses on her face, she opened the bathroom door. The bedroom was empty. "Lucas?"

Why she called him, she didn't know. From where she stood, she could see the entire room. The door suddenly swung open, and Lucas strode in, shirtless, carrying the ice bucket and juggling something in his shirt.

He paused when the door clunked shut and said, "Hi." He dumped his shirt on her bed and out tumbled a wide selection of junk food. He must've spent twenty bucks in the vending machine. He set the ice bucket on the nightstand between the beds. It held a couple bottles of pop and some water. "I figured we'd get hungry. Did you pick out a movie?"

"Uh, no. I just got out of the shower and was wondering where you'd gone."

He shook out his shirt, and she tried unsuccessfully not to stare. He bunched it up and slid his arms through while her mouth watered over the insanely sexy muscles. She bit her lip to stop herself from drooling. This would do nothing to prevent the rampant fantasies that would accompany what she'd imagined in the shower. Her skin warmed at the thought.

Lucas walked past her, oblivious to her thoughts, and said, "Cute glasses."

She touched them self-consciously. "Thanks."

He jumped onto his bed and patted the spot beside him. "Come on. Let's get a movie going."

Felicity looked over her snack choices and grabbed a bag of corn chips and M&M's. "What do you want?" she asked, pointing at the pile.

"Whatever."

She couldn't believe he didn't care. No one was that laid back, but he really didn't seem to have a preference. She tossed him a bag of potato chips and debated whether she should sit on her bed.

Lucas scooted over a little more. "Sit here."

So she did. He clicked through the movie options, and she quickly chose a romantic comedy while trying to block out the warmth of his body beside her. He lay close enough that when they opened their bags of chips, their arms bumped. If she shifted her leg a half inch to the right, she'd be able to feel the hair on his legs, so she locked every muscle.

The scent of his cologne intrigued her. It was a total man cologne—nothing flowery for this guy. It was a sandalwood base, but she couldn't grab the middle notes. She made a mental reminder to check the bathroom for the bottle later. Scent was something that deeply affected her, mostly because so many people got it wrong. They tended to sniff the bottle, maybe spritz it in the air, but testing it on your own skin was important.

And Lucas had gotten it right.

The opening credits rolled and campy music played. For the next two hours, Felicity was entertained by the movie in front of her and the comments from the man beside her. For once, it wasn't about learning—although she did, thanks to Lucas's constant barrage of "No guy thinks that way"—but she was able to just relax and enjoy the moment.

CHAPTER FIVE

Felicity sat in a chair across from Becky, waiting for the woman to place her breakfast order. The waitress turned away, and Becky refocused her attention on Felicity and Lucas. He'd chosen to sit next to Felicity, which as a couple, she supposed made sense, but it felt like it was more.

Becky leaned her forearms on the table, her perfectly golden skin a contrast to the white tabletop. "So, Lucas, what do you think about this whole destination wedding thing?"

He shrugged. "It works for them, I think."

"But it doesn't seem real, does it? It's like a play or something." She turned her brilliant smile on Felicity. "Do you know what I mean?"

Hell no, she didn't, but Felicity knew better than to say that. "I guess it's a way to keep it small."

"It's a little inconsiderate to your guests, though. To just assume that people can plan a whole vacation and afford to come here."

Lucas responded, "No one said guests had to stay for the week. Besides, this place has special meaning for them."

"You have a point, I suppose, but you know me, Lucas, I want the whole shebang. Big church wedding, long reception with everyone invited." Becky's gaze returned to Felicity.

"Personally, I like the idea of eloping."

Becky's eyes widened. "Eloping? What about your family and friends?"

"A marriage—a wedding—is about the bride and groom. No one else should really matter. It's about the commitment they make to each other." Felicity glanced at Lucas to make sure she hadn't said anything wrong and then took a sip from her water.

"No, I have to disagree with you there, Felicity. A wedding is about *celebrating* your love with your partner in front of witnesses. They all want to share in your joy." Becky waved her hands while she spoke and the sun glinted off the rings on her fingers.

Felicity shrugged. She didn't have an answer for that.

Lucas's arm slid around the back of her chair. "Then you throw a party after the fact."

"Well, it doesn't surprise me that you'd say that."

Felicity looked at him, hoping for some explanation, but received none.

The waitress arrived with their food. Both Felicity and Lucas had a full breakfast with eggs and bacon and toast, while Becky ate oatmeal and a bowl of fruit.

"So, Felicity, what do you do for a living?"

"I'm still in school."

Becky's eyebrows shot up.

"I'm graduating this year." She scrambled to think, and then added quickly, "Harvard." That single word tended to impress people, and it would buy her time to figure out which questions from her list she should use.

"Interesting. And how exactly did you two meet?"

Lucas patted Felicity's leg, their signal that he would answer. "Felicity was home visiting. She's from Chicago. We met at a bar. One look and we pretty much just clicked."

Felicity swallowed hard. Anyone who knew her knew that she never met a guy in a bar, unless Charlie or Layla forced her to. That would work. She would just weave her friends into Lucas's story.

"So what's your degree in?"

"Chemistry."

Becky's face brightened. "Oh, so you'll be a teacher like Lucas."

"God, no." Her comment seemed to surprise Becky. "I mean, I plan to work for my father. He has a spot for me in his research and development department. I make perfume."

"That's interesting."

Another dead end. But then Felicity remembered that Lucas told her to ask questions. "What do you do?"

"I work in a law office. I'm a paralegal, but I'm considering going to law school."

For the remainder of their brief meal, Lucas and Becky discussed some mutual acquaintances, so Felicity tuned out. It seemed as though her presence was enough. Becky excused herself and fumbled with her elegant clutch before Lucas waved her off. "I've got breakfast. See you at the wedding."

He stood, and she went on tiptoe to kiss his cheek. "How long are you staying?"

"My flight leaves on Wednesday."

Hearing the information was like being poked. Felicity hadn't thought about him leaving.

"Maybe we'll see each other after the wedding then." Becky leaned forward. "Felicity, it was nice to meet you."

"You too."

When Lucas sat again, Felicity said, "That went well."

"It did."

"I don't get why you broke up with her. I mean, she's intelligent, beautiful, can obviously carry on conversations with people."

"Who said I broke up with her?"

Felicity pushed her plate away and picked up her coffee. "Even I know that if she did the breaking up, she wouldn't be trying to make a move on you now. Unless of course that's all your delusions, in which case, I should probably leave."

He laughed. His smile was genuine and happy, unlike the one he'd worn throughout breakfast. Something warm tumbled through her with the knowledge that she'd accomplished that.

"Becky is not always what she seems."

"She was totally nice."

He grunted.

"What does that mean?"

"It means that I broke up with Becky because we wanted different things in life. As far as her being nice, not really."

"What are you talking about?"

He leaned his elbows on the table. "You remember the mean girls in high school?"

Now it was Felicity's turn to laugh. She pointed to herself. "Socially inept science nerd. I was well acquainted with all of the mean girls."

"Becky was Queen Bee. And where most girls grow up and out of it, she became better at it." He sighed and leaned back in his chair. He reached over and brushed her hair back on her shoulder. "What you saw as friendliness, I recognized as her sizing you up, trying to figure out how to take you down."

"Take me down from what?"

He shook his head. "I'm not really sure. Are you ready to go?"

"Sure." She stood. "I have to go check in at my hotel before they cancel my reservation. I also need to find a dress to wear tonight. The one I wore yesterday was the only one I packed."

Lucas stepped away from the table, leaving cash behind for the bill. He put his arm around her shoulder. "Make sure you pick out something sexy. I want to make every other man at the wedding jealous."

She laughed again. No one was ever jealous of her.

"Want some company?"

"You want to go shopping?"

"Why not? I've got hours until the wedding. If I stay here, my family will just try to give me things to do."

"Okay."

~

LATER THAT EVENING, FELICITY WAS ACTUALLY having fun. She'd made it through cocktails and dinner, although admittedly having Lucas at her side made it easy. His formula for conversation worked great. Or maybe it was that she'd already had a couple of glasses of wine and felt pretty relaxed. She'd watched Lucas handle small issues as they arose. He didn't comment or complain, just did whatever his family asked of him.

Different girls, especially the bridal party, clamored for his attention too, wanting to dance with him, and he accommodated them all. His smile never faltered. She stood on the edge of the dance floor, feeling self-conscious in the tighter than normal dress in midnight blue that Lucas had not only picked out, but also insisted she get. Her small boobs were pushed up by a built-in bra, and for once in her life, she had cleavage. The back of the dress was cut deep, and she felt her hair swooshing when she walked.

As he finished his dance with the mother of the bride, Lucas caught her gaze. After saying his farewell to the older woman, he made his way to her. "Finally going to give in and dance with me? I promise, no chicken dance."

The DJ took that moment to put on something with a thumping beat, so Felicity shook her head. A slow dance, she could handle. It was mostly swaying. But something upbeat required rhythm. She tilted her head to get him to follow her to a spot where they could talk. She wanted to ask him before she lost her nerve.

She took the final swig of her wine and left the glass on a nearby table. When they were away from most of the guests, she said, "I know what I want."

"Okay."

"You said you owe me, right? For agreeing to be your—"

Suddenly, his mouth was on hers, firm, soft lips pressing against her. Her heartbeat kicked, and she stepped closer, wanting to feel his body. She opened her mouth slightly in invitation, but he pulled away. His face stayed closed to hers as he whispered, "Sorry. I knew where you were going, and I didn't know how else to make you not finish that sentence. You were talking pretty loud."

Oh. He hadn't wanted to kiss her. He wanted to shut her up. She really did need his help. She whispered back, "I want you to teach me to pick up a guy."

Saying it out loud sounded much worse than it had in her head.

"What?"

"You said you owe me. I've been using your formula for small talk at a wedding full of strangers and I'm successful. I've been watching you for two days. People love you. You know how to interact with them, to interpret what they need, what they're trying to say. Teach me to do that."

"You're crazy."

"No, I'm determined. Once this wedding is over, I have no plans and I'm here for a week. I want it to be a real vacation."

He stared into her eyes and became serious. "You mean it. You're not kidding."

"Haven't you figured out by now that kidding isn't a strong suit?"

"You won't have any problems picking up guys, trust me."

"No, you trust me. I can't." She tugged on his shirt to bring him closer to her mouth. "It's been a really long time, if you know what I mean."

His eyes closed, and his jaw clenched as he straightened away from her. He grabbed her hand. "A new song. Let's dance."

"What about our deal?"

"We'll talk about it tomorrow."

"Is that a yes?"

He stared down at her as he pulled her into his arms. "Yes."

Felicity had no idea what she was doing in this man's arms, but it felt good. She'd never been much of a dancer, avoiding school dances and parties because she always felt awkward. But had she known it could be like this, she might've reconsidered.

Lucas towered over her, so she rested a cheek on his chest as his arm came around her back. His palm was slightly rough against the bare skin of her back, while his other hand held hers close to his chest. He smelled amazing, even better than he had last night while they lay in bed watching a silly movie. She'd expected him to talk, but he didn't. He just held her and swayed to music she didn't even hear.

Their dance was interrupted in the final notes by one of the bridesmaids, not Becky, though. Felicity found it fascinating that the one person Lucas had been most worried about stayed clear of him the whole night. Maybe he *was* delusional. As he began the next dance with the other girl, Felicity went back to the bar for another glass of wine.

She normally didn't drink much, but this was really good wine and she was celebrating. Not only was she successfully participating in social engagement, but she also had a tutor for the finer points of picking up guys. She sipped at her glass and thought about the kiss. It had been one hell of a kiss. She definitely wanted more of that.

No, not more of that. More *like* that. Because Lucas had made it clear that he wasn't interested in her that way. Before she knew it, her glass was empty again. She debated getting a refill, but when she saw Lucas still dancing, she opted for the drink. From her corner perch at the bar, she could see the entire dance floor and she enjoyed watching people dance and mingle. She wished she were brave enough to join the crowd.

From the other side of a potted plant, something caught her attention. A voice, a comment, something. She strained to listen and then realized who it was. Becky.

"Oh, please, Lucas isn't serious," she said.

"How can you know that? They were pretty cute dancing together."

"Because Lucas is a fixer. When he discovers that she can't be fixed, he'll be all kinds of disappointed and he'll move on. And when he does, I'll be waiting. He just needed time to realize that he's ready to be with a woman who is complete. This latest little project won't hold his interest for long."

Felicity's jaw dropped. They were talking about her? She was a project? She gulped the rest of her drink and let the words sink in. Could Becky be right?

A small voice in her head agreed. Of course, Becky was right. Felicity had seen Lucas solve problems and fix things for numerous people over the last two days. He fixed her problem with the rental car. He taught her how to carry on small talk with strangers. Hell, she'd asked him to fix her so she'd be able to pick up a guy.

And really, none of that bothered her.

What bothered her most about the whole conversation was the attitude Becky had toward Lucas. As if he was somehow dim-witted for wanting to help people. Becky hadn't seen her, and Felicity didn't give away her position, but when Becky moved toward the dance floor, making a beeline for Lucas, Felicity hopped off her stool. She wobbled a bit and then propelled herself forward.

If nothing else, she was here to keep Becky away from Lucas. That was part of their deal.

Becky's back was to Felicity as she tried to tug Lucas to the dance floor. Felicity only heard the tail end of whatever Becky was saying, and it ended with, "What do you see in her?"

Felicity stepped in between them and slid her arm around Lucas's waist. "I'm absolutely amazing in bed. He's said that he'd never been as thoroughly fucked as he has been with me."

Becky's mouth opened and closed as she stepped back. When Becky was off the dance floor, Felicity took a step away, but Lucas pulled her and she crashed into him. She looked up into his face to apologize, but his smile startled her.

"That was fabulous."

"What?"

"I don't think anyone has ever spoken to Becky that way."

"Sorry. It was crude, but if you could've heard—"

He lowered his head and kissed her again; this time his tongue slid into her mouth, catching her by surprise. He tasted good. The slow stroke of his tongue and the press of his lips made her moan.

He pulled away, and she opened her eyes.

"Are you drunk?"

She shook her head, then squinted. "Maybe a

little. I told you I'm not much of a drinker." She stepped closer, rubbing her body against his, getting even more turned on thinking about the hard muscle beneath the suit he wore.

He ran a finger down the side of her face, the touch gentle. "Thank you for getting rid of Becky. You are the best date I've ever had at a wedding."

"Go to weddings often?"

"Okay, maybe that was a bad choice of words." He put his arm around her shoulder again in a move that was becoming way too comfortable. "Let's go get you some coffee."

She sighed. There went the phenomenal kisses. As they walked to the bar, Felicity wondered if he passed out kisses like that to all the girls or just the ones who pretended to be his date.

CHAPTER SIX

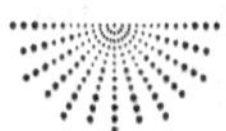

*L*ucas tracked down a waiter and asked for two cups of coffee. Felicity planned to go back to her hotel tonight, so she needed to sober up. It was probably for the best because if she stayed with him, he couldn't guarantee that he wouldn't make a move. Even though she looked so fucking hot in that dress, all he'd wanted to do all night was peel it off her. But she'd made it clear that she was here as his fake date and her goal was to pick up other men on her vacation.

He handed her a coffee. As her lips touched the rim of the cup, he was reminded of their kiss. She'd participated in that kiss. He gave himself a mental shake. She was almost drunk. Of course she participated. Even if she hadn't drunk all that wine, she would've let him kiss her to keep up appearances. She hadn't shied away from his touch once.

But most of the time, she looked at him like maybe he was a little crazy.

She drank the coffee in silence, watching the wedding guests get drunk and attempt to dance. He didn't touch the other cup. He wanted another beer, but figured it wouldn't be nice to drink in front of her when he was telling her to sober up. As soon as she was sober, she would leave.

The thought left him cold. He'd had a great time hanging out with Felicity for the past two days and hadn't given much thought to her not being around tomorrow. "Want to dance?"

She jerked in her seat and turned to face him. "Huh?"

"Dance. Do you want to?"

She sighed. "I'm not a good dancer."

"You danced fine before."

"That was a slow song."

He stood and walked to the DJ to request a slow song. If this was his last chance to hold Felicity, he would make the most of it. By the time he returned to her, the slow song was starting. It was old, Journey, if he wasn't mistaken. He held out his hand, and Felicity stared up at him. "You wanted slow."

She stood, placing her palm in his. "I'm still wobbly."

"That's okay. I won't let you fall."

He led her to the dance floor and pulled her into his arms. She wrapped an arm around his waist and interlocked the fingers of her other hand with his. His right palm rested at the base of her back, right on the curve at the top of her ass. His thumb stroked the skin left bare by the back of the dress. He wondered if he could dip his hand inside but shook the thought away.

"I've had a good time tonight."

"Really?" he asked. She'd been a great sport, putting up with his family asking all kinds of questions and demanding her attention while he dealt with one minor crisis or another. They easily accepted her as his girlfriend, and it might be harder than anticipated to explain to them that he and Felicity had broken up.

She moved her head and tilted her face up. "Yes, really."

Her eyes were clear, honest. He liked that about her. What you saw seemed to be what you got with Felicity. As his gaze locked on hers, their feet barely shuffled. Time froze and their breathing synchronized.

One eyebrow flicked up a moment before Felicity's hand bunched his shirt and tugged him down. "Kiss me."

He didn't need further urging. The hand at her back pulled her closer, pressing her body into his. He wanted to feel the softness of her against him. His lips brushed hers, and her hand grabbed the back of his head, fingers gripping his hair, as her tongue touched his. He tasted the coffee and behind that, sweet wine.

She wasn't waiting for him to take the lead. She demanded his attention. He grabbed her ass and held on. His hard-on pressed against her. She eased away. "Let's go upstairs."

He tore his gaze away from her and looked around the room. The party was winding down, and while his absence might be noticed, he wouldn't be missed. "You sure?"

She nodded.

With his hands, he cradled her face and stared into her eyes carefully assessing her. "I'm not asking if you want to. I'm asking if you're sober enough to want to."

"Yes to all of the above."

He took her hand and led the way to the elevators without a word to anyone. If he said good-bye, it would turn into long conversations that would ruin the momentum. They stepped into the elevator, and Felicity yanked his tie loose. She began to unbutton his shirt and nudged her body between his legs. As she kissed his chest, she rubbed her body against his throbbing dick.

He gripped the rail behind him for balance and willed the car to move faster. When the doors slid open on his floor, he grabbed Felicity's shoulders and pushed her into the hall. "Don't lose that thought." Fumbling in the pocket of his currently too-tight pants, he found the key card and shoved the door open.

By the time he turned on the light, Felicity had already stepped out of her shoes and had contorted her arms to reach her zipper.

"Allow me," he said, skimming his fingers over her bare shoulders and down the deep V of the dress to where the zipper started. He kissed the spot between her shoulder blades. She shivered. The zipper hissed and her breath followed. As soon as the material loosened, she turned to face him, tugging the dress loose and allowing it to drop from her body.

The slick material pooled at her feet, and she wore nothing beneath the dress. He was so grateful he hadn't known that earlier. It would've made functioning damn near impossible. She stepped closer, and he realized he was staring. She finished unbuttoning his shirt and yanked it from his pants.

The process was taking too long. He toed off his shoes and worked the buckle of his belt free. Because his hands were busy, Felicity couldn't get his shirt all the way off.

"Stop moving," she ordered.

He froze. She slid the sleeves off his arms and tossed the shirt aside. Her cool fingers skated along his waistband and finished opening his pants. She slid her palms against his hips and shoved his pants down, taking his boxers with them. She followed with her body until she was on her knees in front of him. His dick was hard and standing out. From her position on the floor, she looked up at him and smiled as she wrapped her cool fingers around his hot flesh and stroked.

His muscles tensed at her touch, and he almost jumped out of his skin when her tongue darted out and wet the tip. He fisted his hands as she took him in her mouth. She moaned, and the vibrations in her throat reverberated through him. He closed his eyes and focused on not embarrassing himself.

With his cock in her mouth, she grabbed his hand and uncurled his fingers before bringing it to her head. Her soft hair tickled his palm. She picked up pace, and his hand tightened on her hair, creating the rhythm he wanted. Fuck, she was hot.

In his head, he began listing baseball stats of his team to hold off exploding. No way was this going to end quickly. But she was insistent, so he pulled away.

"Hey, I wasn't done." She leaned back on her heels.

"Yeah, well, I don't want to be done yet, either, and if you keep going, I will be." He bent over and hauled her to her feet. He kissed her swollen lips and palmed her ass, enjoying the feel of it even more without the barrier of the dress.

"Bed," she said against his lips.

He grabbed her hips and tossed her. She squealed when she went airborne, even though it wasn't far. She laughed and then thumped a fist on her chest. "Ug, me caveman."

"Not a caveman, unless you like that sort of thing. You said you wanted the bed. I take direction well." He turned to his bag to find some condoms.

"Hey," she called. "When I said bed, I expected you to join me."

He turned back to her and held up the condoms. Tossing them on the nightstand, he lay down beside her. He stroked his hand up the outside of her thigh to her hip. She spread her legs, inviting his touch, but he took his time. He caressed the soft skin of her stomach and let his fingertips toy with the trim hair of her pussy.

She grabbed his head and thrust her tongue into his mouth. Her hips wiggled. When he touched her, she was already wet. He rubbed her clit, earning him a deep moan. She ground against his hand, creating her own rhythm. He raised himself up on one arm and reached for a condom.

She snatched it from him and ripped it open. She gave his shoulder a quick shove to get him to lie back. Once the condom was in place, she climbed on top of him and began to ride. She bounced hard and fast as he held her hips. Her eyes were closed, and she grabbed her breasts and squeezed, tugging at the nipples.

He just watched her, getting more turned on at the sight, until he couldn't take it anymore. He sat up, holding on to her back, so she wouldn't fall. Her eyes popped open like she'd forgotten he was even part of the equation.

Her hands fell away, and he sucked a nipple into his mouth. He shifted to the edge of the bed, giving him more control of her thrusts. He slowed her pace, drawing out the pleasure for both of them, until she was pulling his hair and slapping his shoulder.

He stood, and her legs automatically wrapped around him. He laid her on the bed, but kept his feet planted on the floor. He hooked an arm under her knee, opening her to him even more. He pounded into her, flesh slapping, breath panting, sweat-slicked skin sliding. Her hand slid between them, and he felt her finger rubbing herself when they collided.

She kept her eyes open, staring at him, dark and full of lust. Her other hand pinched a nipple, and she smiled at him. He leaned over, feeling her muscles contract, and kissed her neck against her throbbing rapid pulse.

She cried out when she came, and he followed, emptying into her, straining every muscle in his body, until he collapsed.

Felicity may have meant her tossed-off comment to Becky to be fiction, but he began to believe Felicity could deliver. He couldn't catch his breath, and he still saw stars behind his eyelids. If he wasn't in such good shape from working out with the baseball team, he might be convinced he was having a heart attack.

Lucas forced himself up on his elbows, worried that he might be suffocating Felicity. She was looking up at him, her chest heaving as much as his. Her eyes were at half-mast, looking sleepy and satisfied. He moved her sweaty hair away from her face, the bouncy curl that she'd put in earlier gone, leaving behind a gentle wave.

"Why are you staring at me?" she asked.

"I like the look of you."

She sat up, forcing him away from her. She ran a hand through her hair and looked around the room. He knew that look. He'd used that look. The one that said, "Where's my shit so I can get going?"

"Don't leave."

She stiffened at his touch on her back. She was ready to bolt, but he had no idea why. What they just experienced was amazing. He continued with something that would work for her: logic. "You might feel better, but you still have a lot of alcohol in your system. You're not good to drive."

She inhaled deeply and slowly released the breath.

He sat up and kissed her shoulder. "Stay with me."

FELICITY WOKE, AND THE SKY WAS JUST BEGINNING to lighten. She looked over at Lucas lying spread eagle, sound asleep beside her, and felt like an idiot. She'd learned her lesson about spending the night with guys. She never understood their intentions or expectations beyond having sex. Sex, she understood.

But something felt different with Lucas. She didn't know why it felt different or if she was even right in her assessment. All she did know was that she didn't want him to wake up and have some stupid conversation about their fake relationship as he tried to let her down easy. She couldn't stomach that.

Because of whatever it was that was different.

She eased off the bed. He didn't stir. Glad she hadn't brought her bag when she checked into her hotel yesterday, she dug through it for clean clothes. She grabbed the dress from last night and shoved it into the bag. Looking around the room for anything else she might've left behind, her eyes landed on Lucas again and she sighed.

He was heading back to Chicago, and she had

a vacation to finish. She really hoped Layla's car was fixed and she was on her way. For once, Felicity would be able to swap stories about phenomenal sex with a random guy.

Even if Lucas no longer felt random.

She left the hotel room, closing the door quietly. The elevator couldn't move fast enough. Even if Lucas didn't wake, he had friends and family all over the hotel that she didn't want to run into. She walked to her car as quickly as possible and drove to her hotel.

In her room, she dropped her bag on the bed and took a long hot shower to try to get Lucas off her mind. After getting redressed, she texted Charlie to see how her weekend went. While trying to figure out her next move, her phone rang. Layla.

"Hello."

"Hey, what's up? You in Texas?"

"Yes, I'm here and it's beautiful. Are you going to make it?"

"I don't think so. Phin said it'll take a couple of days to fix my car. Best case, it'll be done on Wednesday. By the time I drive there, it would be time to turn around and head back to school."

Felicity's stomach sank. "No. That's awful. What am I supposed to do?"

"What do you mean? Have fun. You're capable of doing this, Felicity. Whenever you're presented with an opportunity, don't do what you would normally do. Stop and think, 'What would Charlie and Layla want me to do?' Then do that."

Felicity groaned, but she had in fact done just that when Lucas asked her to go to the wedding.

"Speaking of Charlie, have you heard from her?"

"She texted yesterday about having dinner with Ethan, but she hasn't responded to my text today to tell me what happened."

"Wait a minute. You're on vacation at a beach, and instead of going out and enjoying yourself, you're sitting there texting Charlie and talking to me? Leave the hotel room."

"I left earlier." Felicity walked out onto the balcony and looked at the beach. It was still early enough that it wasn't yet crowded.

"For breakfast, right?"

Felicity didn't respond. Part of her wanted to tell Layla about Lucas, but in truth, she didn't know what to say.

"Put on your swimsuit, pack a bag, and leave. Promise me that you won't go back to your room for at least the next six hours."

A jolt of panic struck her. "What am I supposed to do for six hours?"

"Swim, sunbathe, drink, pick up a gorgeous guy, eat, drink some more, make friends."

The thought of last night's wine made her cringe. "That's a lot of stuff I'm not good at."

"Promise."

"I'll try."

"Do or do not. There is no try."

Felicity laughed. "Don't you think it's time to let go of the *Star Wars* quotes?"

"Blasphemer. Go have fun. I plan to."

"I'm sure you do." Felicity's voice held a hint of jealousy. "How did you meet this guy?"

Layla told her about Phin, and Felicity was surprised by how much Layla knew about him in such a short time. Then she thought about Lucas again. "Are you falling for this guy?"

"I don't know. I've only known him for a couple of days."

"But you're talking like you're all invested in his life. If it was just sex, then that's all you'd be rambling on about. Don't get me wrong, I'm kind of glad you're off that conversation, since I have none coming my way, but you have to know that this can't go anywhere."

"I'm not doing anything crazy. I'm enjoying my spring break. Phin is not a long-term any-thing. He's moving on himself soon. Heading to Vegas and who knows where after that." Layla sighed. "I really needed a vacation. That's what I'm doing here," she told Felicity. "Spring break. Our last one. I only wish we were together. I found my fling. You need to go get yours. Then we'll talk next week and compare notes."

"I love how you tell me to just 'get one,' as if I've ever been able to do that."

"You can do it. Channel Charlie. That girl will get you laid faster than anything."

Again she was tempted to tell her about Lu-cas, how she'd gotten laid all on her own, but it made her kind of sad because to her it was more than getting laid. And then she'd snuck out of his room.

"Good luck."

Felicity laughed. It was her turn to toss out a quote. "Captain, you almost make me believe in luck."

"I can't quote Yoda, but you can quote Spock? I don't think so."

"Give me a call if you need anything." Felicity settled in the chair and put her feet up on the rail. The sun warmed her skin, and she knew she needed to put on sunblock, but for a few minutes, she just wanted to be.

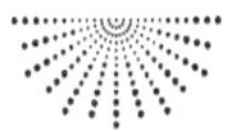

CHAPTER SEVEN

*L*ucas rolled over and felt nothing. He opened his eyes and saw light creeping past the edge of the curtain, but no Felicity. He turned to the bathroom. Light off, no noise. She was gone. He sat up and noticed her bag was missing. Why would she leave like that? He knew she'd planned to leave last night, but she didn't say anything. They fell asleep together, and while they didn't cuddle, they touched all night.

A rock settled in his stomach.

She'd said she wanted to pick up guys. Maybe that's all she wanted was a one-night stand. He scrubbed a hand over his face. He had her number, but how awkward was that? Desperate didn't look good on him.

He showered and dressed, and when a knock sounded at his door, his heart thumped in hope. Maybe Felicity had just stepped out for breakfast and came back. He swung the door open, trying to look cool, only to be facing his mother. "Hi, Mom."

"I'm glad you're awake. We're all heading down to lunch." She not too subtly looked around the room. "Where's Felicity?"

"Out. She wanted to go do some stuff." Yeah, that sounded convincing.

"Too bad. I was hoping to talk with her some more. The two of you cut out a little early last night." She gave him a knowing look.

"We're both adults."

"I know. Which is why I wasn't knocking on your door last night after you disappeared." She reached out for his arm. "Come on. I want to hear more about this girl who stole your attention."

He'd hoped to avoid this. He knew he could fool Becky, and even his brother, with his charade with Felicity, but moms were always a different story. They could sniff out a lie a hundred feet away. He allowed her to lead him down the hall as he thought about Felicity. "What do you want to know?"

"Whatever secrets you want to share."

This was something he liked about his mom. She'd prod, but not pressure.

"She's pretty amazing." As soon as the words left his mouth, he knew them to not only be true, but he also knew that he wouldn't have to lie. He did know quite a bit about Felicity. "She's a chemistry major and plans to work for her dad making perfume."

"She told me that. I want to hear why you like her." The elevator doors swooshed open.

They stepped in and Lucas thought. "She's really smart. And intense. Like when she's focused on something, there's no distracting her." At least not that he'd been able to find, but it sure would be nice to try. "She's shy and not very good with people."

"What makes you say that? Everyone who spent time with her yesterday made a point of asking me when the next wedding was taking place."

Wow. He knew Felicity had felt comfortable, but he wasn't aware that she'd made such an impact. Not that he should be surprised because she'd been determined.

His mother's voice broke into his thoughts. "She will be joining us for dinner, won't she?"

He shook his head clear as the doors opened to the lobby. "What dinner?" Panic bit into him. He hadn't thought any further than the reception.

"I told you yesterday. We're having a farewell dinner tomorrow night since the newlyweds are staying the week, but the rest of us are going back."

He didn't remember any such conversation or he would've brought it up to Felicity. "Aren't the newlyweds sick of us? I would think they'd be locked in their hotel room with a 'Do Not Disturb' sign posted for days."

"It was their idea. They want to keep celebrating."

"I don't know, Mom. Felicity's already been stuck doing family stuff with me. This is her spring break. She wants to have fun."

The stone returned to his stomach as he thought of her having fun with other guys.

"Call her now and ask."

He sighed. This was a test. Mom knew something was up. As he followed her to her car, he dialed Felicity's number. It went to voice mail, so he left a message that he hoped didn't sound too awkward since his mother was still within earshot. He couldn't say what he really wanted to, which was frustrating.

When his mother looked at him expectantly, he shrugged. "She didn't answer. She's probably sprawled on the beach somewhere."

The image of Felicity in a swimsuit flashed in his head.

Over the top of the car, his mom shot him a look. "The real question is, why aren't you with her?"

He offered another shrug and slid into the car. When she got behind the wheel, he said, "I overslept. Too much drinking and stuff last night."

"Hmm-mm." Yeah, that was a mom sound all right.

All during lunch, he prayed for his phone to vibrate in his pocket. He didn't even care if Felicity agreed to come to dinner; he just wanted to hear her voice, find out why she left so suddenly. Try to talk her into sleeping with him again. The last thought overshadowed all the rest.

He'd made sure he sat far from Becky, who kept smiling at him from the other end of the table. In order to keep from saying anything, he kept remembering the look on Becky's face when Felicity had told her about fucking him. No one would've guessed a comeback like that would come from Felicity because she looked so timid.

After sleeping with her, however, he knew better. She wasn't timid. She controlled every moment and took what she wanted. He was getting turned on just thinking about her.

"Where's your girlfriend, Lucas?" Becky yelled across the table. The woman couldn't just let him be.

"She went to the beach."

"We should all get together later and go to a club or something."

He snorted. He couldn't picture Felicity in a noisy club surrounded by the pressing bodies of strangers. She didn't even like to dance. "I think we're busy."

"Come on. You're not newlyweds hiding out. Have some fun."

Fun and Becky didn't go hand in hand. Not for him and certainly not for Felicity. He pushed away from the table and set his napkin down. He walked over to where Becky sat. Leaning down, he quietly said, "I have zero desire to socialize with you." He straightened and looked to his mother. "I'll be waiting outside."

He walked out into the heat and humidity. The scorching sun glared, and he looked for a bit of shade to stand in while waiting for his mom. Dinner tomorrow night was a bad idea. But spending more time with Felicity wasn't. He held his phone in his hand and debated calling again.

Felicity listened to the message again and tried to figure it out. Lucas's voice came across the line. "Hey, Felicity. I know you're off enjoying the beach, but my mom just told me about a dinner tomorrow night that she'd like you to join us for." She heard him heave a sigh. "I know you're probably fed up with my family, but I told her I'd ask. She didn't want me to wait until later."

She stared at the screen as the timer ticked its way toward the end of the message. What the heck did that mean? Lucas sounded weird, so unlike his friendly, easygoing voice. He'd said he only needed her to be his date for the wedding. Why would he ask about dinner tomorrow? She mulled over his words again and finally realized that his mom was probably standing right there listening as he made the call. It would certainly explain why he hadn't mentioned her sneaking out after having sex.

Leaning back in her chair on the balcony, she stared out at the water. Shade covered most of her body, but the sun beat down on her legs up on the rail. Again, she thought of sunscreen. She should also leave her room like she promised Layla she would. Not that sitting in the sun and thinking about her night of fabulous sex was a horrible way to spend her day.

She closed her eyes and thought about Lucas and whether he really expected her to call back when her phone vibrated against her chest. Picking the phone up, she squinted at the screen. Lucas. Her chair crashed back down on all four legs and her heart thudded. She stood before hitting the button. "Hello?"

"Hey, Felicity, it's Lucas."

She rolled her eyes. "I have caller ID."

"Sorry. I just wanted to apologize for the message earlier."

He still sounded weird. "Is your mother making you call me again?"

He laughed and she relaxed. "No. I'm glad you could tell she put me up to that call. We went out to lunch and everyone was looking for you. You made quite the impression last night."

She closed her eyes with a groan and thought of the many ways she might've embarrassed him as she sank back to the chair. Her comment to Becky led the list. Becky had probably already shared her crude remark with everyone just to prove how "unfixable" she was.

"What was that for? Everyone loved you."

Her eyes popped open. "What?"

"Everyone who spoke to you loved you. They said things like you're a charming girl."

She laughed. And laughed. And then laughed some more until she doubled over. Lucas's voice murmured in her lap where she'd dropped her phone, bringing her back to reality. She scooped up the phone and placed it against her ear. "I'm here," she said breathlessly. Grin in place, she took a steadying breath.

"Are you okay?" he asked.

Another slow inhale before responding. "I haven't laughed that hard in forever. Are you serious? Your family loved me?"

"According to my mom, yeah. That's why she wants you to come to dinner tomorrow."

"I guess I'm a pretty good actress then." She paused because she never would've pulled it off if it hadn't been for him. "And you're a miracle worker. No one has ever been able to give me the magic formula for social interaction. Thank you."

"No, thank you. I don't know if I would've survived the wedding without you."

He got quiet suddenly, and her stomach tightened. She stood and braced her elbows on the rail.

"Why did you leave this morning?"

She considered hanging up. She could probably get away with it and just ignore him if he called back. But in her mind, she saw his smiling face, and she didn't want to do that to him.

"Didn't you have fun? I thought it was good for you too."

Crap. He thought the sex wasn't good? She swallowed a chuckle. "Just the opposite. It was amazing."

"Then why sneak out?"

"I wasn't really sneaking." *Liar.* "You looked tired, and I didn't want to wake you. Plus, my commitment to you as your date was officially over."

"Uh-huh."

He didn't sound like he believed her. It was the same sound Charlie and Layla made when they wanted to call her a liar but were trying to be nice.

"I guess I need to hold up my end of the bargain then."

"What?"

"You asked me to help you pick up guys. I'll meet you at your hotel at seven. We'll have dinner and our first lesson."

"But—" Her phone bleeped at her to signify he'd hung up. She plopped back into her chair. What was that about? He had to know that she didn't really expect him to teach her how to pick up guys, especially after last night. Even she wasn't so dense to think that was a good idea.

AT SIX FORTY-FIVE, FELICITY WAS STILL STANDING in a towel looking over her choices for clothes for the evening. Lucas hadn't said where they would be going, and she had no idea how to dress. Damn. This wasn't a date. It didn't matter what she wore. They were having dinner, and Lucas was going to teach her, to try to fix her, which according to Becky, he was quite good at. She doubted she would learn enough to pick up a guy tonight.

And after last night, she wasn't sure if another guy would measure up. She pulled on a skirt that Layla had given her and paired it with a tank top. As she tried to remember where she'd tossed her sandals, she briefly worried that she'd forgotten them in Lucas's room. A knock sounded at her door, and she was still thinking about the sandals when she opened the door to Lucas's smiling face.

"What are you doing here?"

"I know I'm a few minutes early, but I did say seven."

"But how did you know what room?" She stepped back from the door to allow him in.

He followed and closed the door behind him, and she was suddenly aware of how big he was as he stood in front of her. "I was with you when you checked in."

"Oh, yeah." When he stood so close, her brain went a little foggy. She tried to ignore the fact that her bed was only a foot away. This man did delicious things to her hormones.

"Ready to go?"

She scratched her head. "Almost. I can't seem to find my sandals." She turned away to dig under the pile of clothes she'd discarded. "You didn't say where we're going. Am I dressed okay?"

He cleared his throat. "Yeah. It's fine."

She looked at him over her shoulder, but he'd turned away to help look for her shoes.

"These what you're looking for?" he asked.

She turned around. Her sandals dangled from his fingers. "Yes, thank you."

Moving closer, she held out her hand to take them, but he simply said, "Allow me."

He knelt in front of her and slid the first sandal on her foot. She had to use his shoulder for balance because feeling his hot breath on her leg was turning her on. His palm caressed her calf as he settled the shoe in place before he curved his arm around her leg to clasp the buckle.

His touch was sensual without being sexual,

and she closed her eyes to absorb the sensation. He repeated the action with her other foot, and when he stood, he was much too close for comfort. She wanted to grab him and kiss him like she had last night. He stared into her eyes, and she thought for a moment he might kiss her.

But he cleared his throat and said, "Ready for dinner?"

Words fled so she nodded. When he turned his back to leave, she wished more than anything that she could read and understand people, especially Lucas and what he was thinking.

Before they arrived at the elevator, he asked, "Is it okay for us to take your car? I took a cab here."

She hadn't thought about that when he proposed meeting her. She probably should've offered to pick him up. Not that he'd given her much choice. "I've got the keys in my purse."

"Can I drive?"

She looked up at him with a raised eyebrow. "Are you insinuating something about my driving skills?"

He smiled that smile that did wonderful things to her stomach. "Of course not. I prefer to drive."

"You just like to be in charge."

His smile faded. "Yes, I do."

His words caused a shiver to race down her spine. She remembered the way he'd taken over during sex, not giving her a choice in their pleasure. He leaned against the rail in the elevator the same way he had last night. If she didn't know better, she'd think he was doing it on purpose to torment her.

"So what exactly do you hope I can teach you?"

She waited until they were through the lobby and walking toward the parking lot. The night air hadn't cooled significantly, but a nice breeze blew over her skin. "I want to learn how to pick up a guy."

Leading the way to her car, she pressed the fob to unlock the doors and then handed Lucas the keys.

"What makes you think you need help?"

"Because I can't do it."

"You picked me up just fine last night."

She laughed, glad to have the easy nature between them again. "You picked me up on the plane and begged me to be your date. I simply offered to screw you. It's not the same."

He began to cough like he'd choked on something. "Trust me, that method will work on just about any man."

She slapped his arm. "Don't make me sound like a slut."

His forehead wrinkled. "It's not complex like figuring out a relationship. You're attempting to pick up guys while on spring break, which means it won't ever go any farther than here. It's one night for a good time. No slut shaming here."

"This is my trial run. If I mess up, no one will know because this is all temporary. But I can take my skills back home with me." After she spoke, his words sank in. Relationships created here wouldn't go anywhere else. She supposed that answered any questions she might've had about their relationship. "I'm not good in the long term, so I'm focusing on the short term."

Lucas drove the short distance to a restaurant, and when he parked, he rushed around to her side of the car, nearly running into her as she stepped out.

"I would've gotten the door for you."

"I'm capable of opening a door. I do it all the time."

"When you're with a guy, if he wants to be a gentleman, let him."

"Is that supposed to be my first rule or something?"

He swung an arm out to prompt her to move. "Not a rule, really. A suggestion. And it wouldn't be the first because it only works once you've snagged a guy."

"Okay. So I'll file that piece of information away for later use."

He placed his hand on the small of her back, a slight gesture that spread warmth through her. She slid a glance at his arm. "Is that being a gentleman too?"

"Of course."

*L*ucas couldn't focus. Felicity's perfume reached inside him and pulled him along as if he had no brain. At this moment he would do anything he could to touch her in any way. Even if it meant that he pretended to have the gentlemanly intentions of a mentor. Inside, they were taken to a table immediately. The restaurant was full without being overly crowded or cramped. By the time they were done eating, Lucas hoped to convince Felicity to go to a bar with him, under the pretense of practicing her new skills.

They sat and stared at the menus. When the waitress arrived, Felicity looked at him. "Am I allowed to order my own food, or does that fall under the gentleman's purview?"

She spoke sweetly, with just a hint of sting that most people wouldn't have noticed. He couldn't help but smile. "Depends on the date. Do you trust me?"

As soon as the words left his mouth, he realized how serious they sounded, as if he alluded to more than a simple meal. She gave a sharp nod of her head, so he looked up at the waitress. He spoke, being careful not to look at Felicity because he didn't want to give away any hint of nervousness.

"The lady will have the chicken and pasta. Can you please put everything separate? The pasta on one plate with a bowl of sauce on the side and the chicken by itself? I'll have sirloin, medium, with a baked potato. And we'll start with a bottle of wine."

He handed her the menus and rested his forearms on the table. "How did I do?"

Her eyes blinked rapidly, and for a moment he considered she was having a seizure, but then realized it was shock. "How did you know?"

"What to order? That was a simple guess."

"To ask for everything separate."

"I listened to you when you ordered at dinner the other night and yesterday at lunch. I watched how you approached your food at the wedding."

She shook her napkin out, and he knew she did it as a means to develop a response, so he gave her time. "It's a texture thing. I don't like the flavors of my food to mix. If everything is separate, and something feels or tastes funny, I can ignore it and eat the rest."

He'd suspected that was the case. He spent his time with teenagers who did all kinds of weird things with food.

"That's what I need you to teach me. I don't

know how to figure out what people like or don't. What they want."

He brushed aside her concern. "That's just paying attention to people." He stopped. She truly didn't understand. "I've seen you watch people. You see everything. Your eyes focus on the scene in front of you and absorb it all."

She licked her lips in a way she had no idea was seductive and rolled her bottom lip in to bite. "But I can't interpret what I see. That's why I can't pick up a guy. I can't read the signals. But if you teach me to put out the right signals, they'll make the move and I won't have to guess." She paused, and a look of longing stole across her face. "Right?"

He couldn't help himself. He reached out and held her hand. "Sweetheart, all you have to do is flirt in a place like this, anyplace really, and guys will flock to you."

She pulled away from his grasp with a laugh. "I can't flirt. Charlie tried to teach me once. She said I looked like a crazy person off her meds."

Lucas bit back a laugh because he knew she'd be offended. The waitress returned with the bottle of wine and poured a glass for each of them. Felicity eyed the glass.

"After last night, I'm not sure more wine is a good idea."

He smirked. "I don't know. I think last night turned out pretty great."

Where some girls might blush or offer a flirty comeback, Felicity just stared. He sighed. "It was a compliment, Felicity. Agree with me, smile, something to let me know that it was the same for you."

Her lips slowly curved as if she wasn't sure of the movement. The smile stretched until he saw the hint of white teeth behind her pink lips. And just like that, the whole room brightened as if lit by a spotlight.

He sipped his wine in hopes of cooling his throat. The sweet tang slid down, but the taste barely registered. His tongue only remembered the taste of Felicity. "About last night."

"I wasn't drunk, but I was tipsy. I shouldn't have jumped all over you like that."

"It wasn't one-sided, Felicity."

"I know, but I agreed to be nothing more than your fake date, and then I went and made you break your moratorium on women. I should've respected you more than that." She paused, her face serious. "Let's forget it happened and go forward being friends. We make a good team."

He tried to not let the full force of the blow hit him. She thought last night was a mistake. He'd been sure that she ran out because she was scared. It felt like more than a quick fuck to him, but he was obviously mistaken. When had he ever been that off the mark?

It took a moment for him to realize she was staring at him expectantly, waiting for him to agree with what she'd proposed.

"So, you want me to teach you how to flirt? What makes you think I could show you? I'm a guy."

"First, you're a guy, so you can tell me what

guys respond to. Second, you're a teacher, so it's natural for you to tutor me. Third, you successfully gave me a formula for getting through the wedding reception. You said it yourself: People loved me." She settled back in her chair, elbows on the armrests. She would make a damn fine lawyer. Make the argument and let it rest.

He inhaled slowly and thought. Looking past her to the bar, he watched the people interact. Of course he was aware that women flirted; however, he never thought about the how or why things worked on him. Were there universal signals?

Thinking about hanging at the bar with his friends, he knew that yes, in fact, some signals were universal to all men. All men looking to get laid anyway. He allowed the ideas to tumble around in his head for a few moments. Felicity needed a plan, a formula to execute, just like the list of questions with appropriate follow-ups. He couldn't give her a pile of possibilities to sort through.

When he returned his attention to her, she had shifted and taken a sip of wine. She stared at him but said nothing. Her eyes, with their laser focus, were where she needed to start. Her eyes alone could bring any man to his knees.

"I'm thinking, developing a plan. Why don't you tell me what you did today?"

"If you're developing a plan, I don't want to distract you." She took a long drink of wine, and he began to think maybe the wine was a bad idea.

"I'm thinking. I can listen and carry on a conversation while I think."

"I talked to Layla. She's not going to make it. Her transmission needs work, and by the time it's finished, she won't be able to get here. Other than that, I sat on my balcony and enjoyed the sun and the sounds of the waves."

He tilted his head, knowing there was more. She shoved her glass away as if it had offended her.

"I finished some work for school too." She paused, then waved her hand. "Go ahead and tell me how I'm on vacation and I shouldn't be working."

"I won't. You like working from your textbook, right? It makes you comfortable and at ease."

Her eyes widened as she nodded.

"What do you like most about science? Is it the fact that the answers line up and balance in formulas?" He thought he might've pegged her on that. Control. Balance.

She shook her head slowly. "No, that's Layla. She's a math major. She likes knowing how to find the answer. Charlie likes the problem, approaching things in different ways like in a video game—choose your own adventure."

"What about you?"

"I love science because for everything we do know, there are still millions of things we don't. There's always something else waiting to be discovered and understood." Her eyes lit up when she spoke.

Hmm. He hadn't thought the unknown would excite her.

The waitress arrived with their meal, and

Lucas thought about how to teach Felicity to flirt. In a flash, it came to him, much like when he was in the classroom and a student struggled to grasp a concept. Sometimes a new way to explain it just bolted into his brain.

"I have it," he said with a broad smile as he picked up his knife and fork to dig into his thick steak.

"Have what?"

"Your formula."

She stopped cutting her chicken into bite-sized pieces and set her silverware down on the edge of her plate. "What is it?"

"EAST."

"East what?"

"It's an acronym. I think it'll work."

The look she shot him was full of disbelief.

"Eat your dinner, grasshopper. Then I'll teach you, and you'll practice."

Her forehead did that adorable crinkly thing. "Grasshopper?"

"I guess you're not into kung fu movies. How about Padawan?"

This time, she nodded. "I prefer *Star Trek* to *Star Wars*, but I get the reference."

He cut into his steak and mentally developed how to explain the lesson as he would for any other student. While they ate, they discussed her plans for after graduation. He talked about his job, the students he worked with, his baseball team.

He wished he could've talked with her all night. Her brain was fascinating. For as much as she was convinced she was socially inept, she was a fabulous conversationalist once you got her going. She made leaps in the conversation that shouldn't have made sense, but did. It all added to the whole picture of who Felicity was.

When their plates were clear, she leaned forward full of eagerness. "Okay, let's go. What's your master plan?"

"EAST. The first thing you need to know is *E*—eye contact. In general, that will be enough of an invitation for a guy if he's looking."

She snorted at him. "Eye contact? Seriously? And I thought Charlie was nuts talking about the hair flip."

"Trust me. You glance at a guy and make eye contact. Hold it for a few seconds. If he's interested, he won't look away. If the first time doesn't work, look around and land on him again. That's enough of a hint. If he doesn't come over, then he's not interested. Move on."

"So you're telling me that if I make eye contact with some guy standing at the bar, he's going to come over here to talk to me?"

Lucas nodded. "It might not work right now because you're here with me. Most guys won't approach a girl who's taken."

Her jaw dropped.

"You know what I mean. We look like we're together, a couple, on a date." Part of him wished it were true. That Felicity was in fact his date.

"Okay. What's next?"

"*A*—attention. You need to really pay attention when a guy talks to you."

Her eyebrows slammed together. "I pay attention."

He chuckled. "You do too much multitasking. Even now, although you're listening to me, you're also thinking about the next two letters of the acronym, how to put all of this into play, and which of the guys at the bar you might want to try this on."

She shrugged. "It's not my fault you talk slow. I can't control my brain wandering off to other things."

"You can control it a little." He considered that for a minute and wondered if she really could control it. Her brain moved pretty fast. "I have no doubt that it'll happen no matter what, but the guy shouldn't be aware of it. First, when he approaches, angle your body toward him. Show him you're open to his approach. When he introduces himself, he'll probably lead with a question, like asking your name. I know you can handle the Q and A from there. I watched you do it at the wedding."

Lucas leaned forward and refilled their glasses, emptying the bottle of wine. Felicity sipped slowly. She didn't look like she was having anywhere near the fun she had last night.

"Okay, eyes and attention. What else?"

"In truth, you probably won't need anything else, but if you're not sure if the guy can take a hint, you use the last two letters: *S*, smile, and *T*, touch."

Her eyebrow rose at the last word.

He rolled his eyes and shook his head. "Offer

a smile. A real one. Laugh at jokes he makes. We all like to think we're funny. Then when it's comfortable, touch him innocently. I'm not talking about a grope session."

Her eyes darted away.

"Touch his arm, brush your hand against his as you reach for your drink, that kind of thing."

Her gaze returned to his, and he knew something bothered her, but he had no idea what. She nodded slowly. "That's all I need, huh? You make it sound easy."

"For chicks, it is. You just need to sit pretty and wait for guys to fall at your feet. We'll jump at the slightest go-ahead. You ready to go?"

"Where?"

"Let's hit a bar and you can practice."

"You want me to pick someone up now, tonight?"

"No time like the present. We'll choose a bar crowded with spring breakers. You'll have your pick."

She smiled and her eyes brightened. "Okay. What do I owe you for dinner?"

He stood and tossed bills on the table. "Nothing. My treat. I owe you at least that. Besides, after I get you liquored up and flirty, I'm going to talk you into going to dinner with my family tomorrow night."

As she stepped away from the table, she looked up at him. "No liquor necessary. I'll go. It's what any friend would do, right?"

∼

FELICITY DIDN'T KNOW WHAT SHE WAS DOING. SHE was far from stupid, but Lucas made her do stupid things. Why would she volunteer to spend more time with him and his family? Especially knowing that Becky would be there. But after her slight outburst, Becky saw her as competition. That was a new experience. No one had ever been jealous of her before.

All these awkward thoughts floated through her brain as Lucas's hand rested low on her back, guiding her to the car. The touch was innocent, but felt intimate. She kept thinking about his hands roaming her body.

But none of that would help her with her mission for the night, which was to learn how to flirt and actually pick up a guy on her own.

Arriving at the car, Lucas opened the door and smiled at her as she climbed in. Something poked the back of her brain as he walked around the car. She closed her eyes and focused. The smile and the touch did it. Lucas was using his own technique on her. While they'd sat at the table, she had his rapt attention and his eyes never left hers. Was she his guinea pig to test the theory? If so, she was proof that it worked. He'd sucked her in like it was nothing.

As he started the car, Felicity smiled. She had another winning formula. The pleasure she would have telling Charlie about this. If she was successful, which she had to be, she wouldn't have to have discriminating taste like she'd told Charlie. It'd been a lie and Charlie had called her on it, but Charlie thought Felicity was too shy to find a guy.

Lucas drove as if he had a destination in mind. He said nothing, so neither did she. She watched his profile in the dying sun, the shadows making the scruff on his jaw even darker. A sudden pulse of lust shot through her as she thought about that scruff against the sensitive skin of her inner thigh. She tore her gaze away and looked out her window.

Lucas pulled into a crowded parking lot and stopped near the door. "Here you go."

"Aren't you coming in?" Panic struck. She knew she wasn't ready to do this alone. She needed a—what did Charlie call it?—wingman.

"I'll be there, but if we walk in together, most guys will assume we're on a date, remember? You go in, find yourself a seat near the center of the bar. Even if you don't see me, know that I'm there watching."

Felicity eyed the door. Nerves fluttered in her stomach. She hadn't been worried about the wedding because she knew Lucas would be there to rescue her if she screwed up, but here she'd be in the middle of a crowd with no help.

"Go on. I'll be right behind you."

She inhaled slowly, filling her lungs to capacity. Pushing her shoulders back, she pulled the handle on the door.

Lucas tapped her shoulder. Leaning close, he whispered, "You got this."

His breath brushed her ear, and she wanted to lean back against him and feel his breath on her bare skin. She wanted to forget this stupid idea of picking up men and enjoy the next two nights with Lucas. Two amazing nights with him would be enough to satisfy her for the week. Then she could slip back into her normal life.

She closed her eyes and pushed off the seat before she acted on her impulse. Without saying anything to Lucas, she stepped from the car and closed the door behind her. Outside, the air was warm and sticky, but inside the bar the air-conditioning was working overtime. The chilly air made her shiver.

She took a minute to scan the layout of the business. Tall tables filled the bar. People sat elbow to elbow. It seemed like everyone came with friends. She didn't see anyone else flying solo. Sad picture, her life.

Making her way to the bar, she checked out her prospects. Groups of men sat together, and as she walked by, she felt some look up and follow her with their eyes. She impressed herself by recognizing that. Luckily, one chair at the bar was open so she quickly slid onto it. While she waited for the bartender to notice her, she twisted and began her search in earnest. Who would make eye contact with her?

Please let him be normal.

"What can I get for you?" the bartender asked behind her.

She spun back. "Just a Coke, please."

He nodded and grabbed a glass to pour the pop. He smiled as he worked, so Felicity tried her formula on him. She made eye contact, held it, but he didn't do anything other than slide the glass in front of her on a napkin. He was either uninterested, or she was already doing it wrong. With her glass in hand, she turned back to the crowd. No one seemed to notice her now.

She glanced at each table, waiting to see if anyone would look up. At the third table, one guy made eye contact. She smiled, hoping it looked like an invitation. He straightened from his position of leaning on the table with his friends, and her stomach did a little flip. He wasn't really her type with his skinny build and blond hair, but this was a trial run. It wasn't like she was really planning to sleep with this guy.

Just when she thought Mr. Blond was going to come over to talk to her, he shifted to look in the opposite direction. Shoot. She moved on, assessing guys at each table, skimming past the groups of women. She stirred her straw in the glass, swirling the ice around before taking a sip.

At this rate, she'd need something a whole lot stronger to make it through the night. A sensation tingled on her neck letting her know someone was checking her out. She turned her chair a little farther to the right to see who it was.

Her heart dropped. Lucas sat at a table by himself with a bottle of beer in front of him. He watched her intently. She pleaded for help with her eyes. Of course, he took pity on her. He pulled out his phone, and a second later, hers was vibrating in her purse.

Setting her drink on the bar, she retrieved her phone.

Don't stare. It makes you look like a stalker. Glance and move on. If you're interested, return after a minute or two.

Jeez, Charlie was right. She did look like a crazy person. She closed her eyes, rallied whatever strength she had left for this mission, and tried again.

CHAPTER NINE

*L*ucas watched Felicity's eyes flutter closed. He tried to reconcile this image of her, one where she appeared unsure of herself, with the woman who climbed all over him in bed last night demanding everything she could from him. She had no idea the power she held. If she figured out how to harness it, no man would be safe.

She reopened her eyes and tilted her head as she scanned the crowd. Her dark hair cascaded down the side of her face brushing the tops of her breasts. He closed his fists on the table as his palms felt the imprint of her nipples as he thrust into her last night.

Focus, Lucas. Felicity wants something else. Just like every woman you fall for.

The thought settled into his brain. Was he falling for Felicity? They'd known each other a few short days. He could easily call her a friend, just as she pointed out earlier. But the thought of her actually picking up some guy tonight and taking him to her hotel bugged the shit out of him. If they were only friends, he knew he shouldn't feel that way.

He drained his bottle of beer and studied Felicity as she tried to make eye contact with a few guys. They had no idea what they were missing. Only five more minutes passed before he saw the frustration on her face. She hopped off her stool, tossed money on the bar, and headed his way.

Slapping her purse on the table, she blurted, "Let's get out of here. Your plan isn't working. I give up."

He smiled. "I never figured you to be one to throw in the towel so quickly."

"I think your formula is off."

"Maybe it's just the application of the formula."

Instead of his joke making her smile, she frowned. "Probably."

Shit. He hadn't meant it like that. "I was kidding, Felicity. It takes practice. Besides, maybe these are the wrong guys for you."

"No guy is wrong when you're just looking to pick him up for the night."

"Why is that?"

She finally sat across from him, and he waved the waitress over. He wanted to hear Felicity's story.

Confusion filled her face. "Like you said earlier, it doesn't matter because every guy has the same parts, the same urges."

He shook his head. "No, I meant why are you only looking for a hookup? Why not Mr. Right?"

"Relationships don't work well with me."

The waitress swung by their table, and Lucas ordered himself another beer and gestured to Felicity. "The same," she answered.

"You drink beer?"

"Sure, why not? The first time I ever got drunk was on beer with Charlie and Layla at Charlie's house. We played a card game—Up and Down the River. I won. We were all drunk, but they were puking."

"Do you have a picture of them?"

"Who?"

"Charlie and Layla. You always talk about them, and I'd like to have an image in my head."

That same unsure look crossed her face. Then she shook her head and reached in her purse. She scrolled through her phone and then handed it to him. "The blonde is Charlie, the other one is obviously Layla."

Lucas stared at the picture. They were by far the sexiest group of nerds he'd ever laid eyes on. Layla and Charlie were pretty, but he couldn't take his eyes off Felicity. In this photo she was undeniably happy. Charlie's smile held a bit of mischief. "It was Charlie's idea to get drunk."

"Yeah. How did you know?"

"She's got the look of a troublemaker."

Felicity laughed. "She is, but it's the best kind of fun."

The waitress dropped off their beer, and Lucas paid her. They wouldn't be staying for more than this one. He didn't want Felicity to get drunk tonight.

He handed her the phone back. "So tell me something about your family."

"I'm an only child. Both of my parents are scientists. My mom works at Fermilab, and my dad has his own perfume company."

"Does he expect you to come work for him, or is it your choice?"

"That's a weird question. Why wouldn't it be my choice?"

"You know, in some families, there's pressure to do certain things, be a certain way." He'd known kids stuck like that growing up. He definitely saw it much too often in his students.

Her bottom lip pushed out. "Nope. They never told me I had to do anything. I mean, they influenced me by buying me chemistry sets when I was little, but they let me try anything I asked. I just fell in love with science."

"Just in your blood, huh?"

She shrugged. "Why are you a teacher?"

"I like kids." He debated whether to leave it at the simple answer or give her the whole truth. She'd moved closer, leaning her forearms on the table, her focus solely on him. Yeah, as soon as she figured out how to harness this, other guys were goners. "I had problems as a kid. Learning problems. School was hard. When I was really young, I was cute and charming, so I talked my way out of or through the work. Later, I struggled with everything, so I acted out. It took a while, but once I got the help I needed, I figured it out, and school wasn't so bad anymore."

He drank from his beer. He rarely talked

about his reasons for becoming a teacher. People usually didn't ask. Conversations tended to be flippant about how easy the job was with short days and summers off. He looked at Felicity, expecting to see a hint of pity, but saw only interest, so he continued. "I had a high school teacher that made everything click for me. He gave me the skills and strategies I needed so I wouldn't feel stupid. Before then, I mostly relied on my charm to get by. He taught me that I was smart enough to handle school."

"I can't even imagine that. School was always easy for me. I never had to work hard at it."

He'd known that. Back on the plane while she scribbled in her notebook working through some impossibly long equation, he'd known she was brilliant.

Her forehead wrinkled. "That was insensitive, right? I probably sounded like I was bragging. I'm sorry."

"You never need to apologize for being honest. I also didn't need you to tell me that you're smart. Looking at the equations you were doing made me dizzy." Again, he took a drink and waited for a reaction, but got none.

"Well, if I could learn to have your ease with people, I'd trade my book smarts in a minute."

He studied her and wasn't sure what to say. Her comment made him realize the reason he was so drawn to her. They both had problems, they could empathize with each other, but it never got in the way of them having a good time. "What do you say we get out of here?"

She glanced at her near-full bottle of beer.

"I'll take you back to your room and help you practice. Part of why my formula isn't working is that you're stiff and forcing it. You need to relax. When we're alone, you're relaxed." He wanted to add that he could help her relax, but didn't want to scare her off. If things progressed in that direction, he wouldn't stop them, but he wouldn't force it either.

She smiled and nodded. "You're right. You put me at ease. I can't even figure out how you do it, but you do. I wish you could just sit at the bar with me."

He opened his mouth to answer, but she put up a hand. "I know, we end up looking like a couple. I guess a few days of faking it makes a lasting impression. Let's go. Are you okay to drive?"

"Yeah, I'm good."

They drove the short distance to her hotel in silence. He liked that he didn't have to be on stage with her. The silence was easy. As he parked, he remembered the part of their conversation he wanted to dig into deeper, that the waitress had interrupted. He wanted to know why she was looking for one-night stands.

He waited until she let them in her room. She started picking up clothes and piling them on the dresser. He eyed the bed, but restrained himself from pulling her into him.

"So how do you want to do this?"

He almost choked at her question. She had no idea what he'd been thinking and how her question sounded to his ears. "Why don't relationships work for you?"

"What do you mean?"

"At the bar. You said that you're not looking for Mr. Right because relationships don't work for you. Why not?"

She sat on the corner of the bed, the mattress dipped slightly. She interlocked her fingers tightly before continuing. "I haven't had many relationships. The few I've had didn't last long. Short term, I'm good. It's just when a guy…"

A bad feeling sank into stomach. He shoved his hands into his pockets and waited, but she didn't continue. "When a guy what?"

"When he spends more time with me, he realizes that I'm not like Layla and Charlie. I'm not fun. I'm not charming. I'm obsessive when I work and I make stupid comments in public and I offend people without trying. Often I spend too much time in my own head. Those issues are hard to overcome long term."

"I think you're wrong. I mean, you're all of those things—the good and the difficult—in your own way."

She snorted at him. "Don't start being politically correct now. I don't need you to spare my feelings. I need a lesson on flirting."

The moment was over. His chance to get her to understand that he knew how special and different she was passed. He sighed, took her hand from her lap, and led her over to the chair by the window. "Sit here like you're at a bar." He scooped up the other chair and carried it across the room.

He angled it so they weren't completely facing each other, but he could see her over his shoulder. "Now draw my attention."

She leaned forward, resting one arm on the table, the other casually over her crossed legs. He didn't face her, but felt her gaze hit him. He paused and waited for the feeling to fade. It didn't. He spun in his chair. "That's the first problem. Don't stare at me to get me to look at you. Look once, look around, and then come back to me. Only hold your gaze on me for a few seconds. I'll feel the attention and turn to see."

She shook out her hands and rolled her neck. "Okay. Like how many seconds? Five, ten?"

"Three the first time and then five the second. It lets a guy know that you're not just casually looking, but interested." He shifted back in his seat. He tried to block his awareness of her to gauge how well she was doing, but he failed. He glanced over his shoulder in time to make eye contact with her. She held it a beat and then her gaze shot to the far wall.

"Okay, once you have my attention, I need an invitation. That's when you flash a smile. It might take a couple of tries, but once you know you have me, smile. Let me know you want me to come over and introduce myself."

She licked her lips and then pressed them together. She was still relaxed, so much more than she had been at the bar, so he turned around again and waited. He looked over his shoulder, and when their eyes met this time, a spark zipped through him. He stared and forced breath into his lungs.

Her lips curved, and she tilted her head slightly, looking at him through lowered lids. The smile was innocent but hinted at all kinds of trouble, and he forgot how to breathe. His mouth returned the smile and he stood.

When he reached the end of the bed closest to her, he sat. "Hi, I'm Lucas. Can I buy you a drink?"

She bit on her lower lip. "Sure, I'd like that."

"You're much better at this than you let on," he whispered.

She uncrossed her legs and scooted to the edge of her seat. "Good at what?" she whispered back, smile still in place.

He knew she was toying with him, but her dark brown eyes were soft and warm, her smile genuine. How could he *not* get pulled under her spell? "Good at this." He waved a hand between them.

She inched forward again and placed a hand on his knee. "You're better."

His body leaned forward of its own volition. Mere inches separated their mouths, and he desperately wanted to taste her again. He began to close his eyes, but she jumped up.

"I did it! Your formula works." She started to pace in the small room, and he wondered how he managed to fuck that up.

"I mean, of course, you knew what I was supposed to do and maybe you guided me a little, but it worked. I felt it. It wasn't forced like it was at the bar."

He stood and followed her movements, willing his hard-on to go away. She jumped at him and wrapped her arms around his neck. He grasped her hips to keep her from feeling how turned on he was, but it was too late. Felicity's body fully collided with his.

His fingers flexed on her hips briefly before clearing his throat and taking a step back. "Uh, good job."

He let his hands slide away. She stared up at him, her cocky grin gone. Her brown eyes darkened and she stepped closer. She gripped his shirt where it met his shorts.

She licked her lips as her fingers skimmed his skin. Blood pounded and his hard-on throbbed. He lowered his head and forced himself to move slowly, to taste her lips and be gentle. He tasted the tang of beer on her tongue as his swept in.

Her eyes closed and she moaned. She rocked against him. Her skirt rode high as she thrust one thigh between his and hiked the other leg and hooked it behind him. Lucas pulled away from her lips and dragged his mouth down her neck. He bit the delicate skin where her pulse beat a rapid tattoo.

The warmth of her skin heightened the scent she wore and it drove him insane. Like a drug, it called to him.

He reached under her skirt and stroked her. God, she was already so wet. He continued to kiss across the neckline of the tank top she wore.

"Stop," she said breathlessly.

Lucas froze, his lips hovering over her nipple that was protruding through the cotton.

Felicity was panting, and she shoved his shoulder to get his attention. When he looked into her eyes, she said, "I don't mean stop. I mean, I need us naked. I need you. Now."

He didn't need any more urging. He pushed Felicity onto the bed and stripped. She watched him from beneath lowered lids. Her body lay sprawled, her limbs loose.

Lucas grabbed her foot and unbuckled the sexy sandal. With the shoe gone, he ran his hand over her calf and up her thigh, stopping short of home plate. He repeated the action with her other foot, and as he stroked the similar path up her leg, Felicity whimpered. He pulled her panties off, his fingers gliding along her sensitive skin.

She curled herself up and yanked off her top and then her bra. She lay back wearing only the small skirt bunched at her waist. He knelt on the bed between her spread thighs. He covered her body with his, lowering his head to take a stiff nipple into his mouth. She arched up to him, her wet center sliding against his cock and a wave of dizziness struck him.

With his hands on her hips, he pressed her into the mattress and kissed his way down her torso. He skipped over her skirt and ran his tongue along her wet slit, swirling around her clit. Her thighs twitched under his forearms.

"Oh, God." It was barely a whisper from her lips.

He nudged her thighs farther apart and settled between them. The scent of her arousal was better than any perfume she could spritz on. He lapped at her and then thrust his tongue inside her, which earned him another moan. He pressed his tongue flat against her clit, and her hands grabbed his head, pulling his hair as she bucked her hips up trying to control his movements.

He pressed his shoulders into her thighs and reached up to her breasts. He pinched a nipple while stroking her with his tongue. Her chest rose and fell so rapidly and her hips wiggled. Her body began to writhe beneath him. He plunged two fingers into her, and her body lifted off the bed with a scream.

As much as he was enjoying playing with her body, he needed to be inside her. His cock throbbed so badly it was nearly painful. He sucked her clit into his mouth one last time and then pulled away.

Felicity gasped and her hands flopped on the bed. Her eyes opened and she stared at him. He yanked the condom from his pants and put it on. Then he crawled back over her body and slid into her.

On a sigh she wrapped her legs around him and he drove deeper. He relished in the wet heat of her. He buried his face in her neck and inhaled before thrusting. She began the rhythm against him, teasing him out of her body.

"God, please, Lucas, move. Faster."

He refused her request. He slid almost completely from her body and then pushed back in, his own body screaming for speed. But she was on the brink, desperate for release and he wanted to draw it out. He needed her to be aware of him bringing this pleasure to her, unlike last time, where she had simply taken it.

Lucas pushed up on his elbows and scraped the hair away from her face. Her eyes were closed in concentration. "Felicity, open your eyes."

Her lids fluttered and she looked up at him. "Stay with me." He thrust deeper and pulled out. As he slammed into her again, her eyes started to close. "Uh-uh. Open, Felicity. It's me and you."

FELICITY FORCED HER EYES OPEN, BUT IT WAS SO hard. The pleasure sang through her body, and she couldn't control her hips. Everything was too much. Lucas, big and overbearing above her, muscles flexing around her. The rasp of his leg hair rough on her inner thighs. The delicious hard length of him pushing into her. Her entire body vibrated with need.

But looking into Lucas's eyes undid her. This was more than just different. It was special, but she didn't even know how or why. She wanted to close her eyes and enjoy the pleasure of the moment, but Lucas wouldn't let her. He was so close. She leaned up and kissed him. His mouth was gentle, his lips barely brushing hers.

He began to move faster, the friction of their bodies making Felicity crazy. Bracing on one elbow, Lucas reached between them and rubbed her clit as he collided with her. She saw stars as her entire world exploded. Waves rolled through her and she clung to him, wrapping as much of herself around him as she could so she had something to hold on to.

Lucas stilled against the spasms of her body and just held her. His face came back into focus, and he smiled at her. Then he began to move at a frenetic pace looking for his own release, but he never closed his eyes or looked away from her.

The muscles in his neck bulged and corded as he growled and bared his teeth. She felt him pulsing in her, against her. He pumped a few more times and then rested his forehead against hers. Sweat dripped from his face. One arm came up and swiped at it. His body pressed on her, though he didn't quite collapse. He finally broke eye contact by nuzzling her neck just below her ear.

Her legs slid away from his hips and landed on the bed, and she focused on getting her lungs to function properly. Lucas rolled off her, sticky sweat smearing across their bodies, a sucking sound where he'd pulled out of her.

She felt spent and useless. For a blissful minute, her mind was blank.

Lucas stirred. He stood and went to the bathroom. In that moment, panic speared into Felicity. What the hell happened?

He came back from the bathroom and she sat up. He needed to leave. This would've been better if they were in his room because then she could leave. How do you tell a guy to get out?

He sat on the edge of the bed, and Felicity did her best to ignore the glorious nakedness of his body. He looked almost as stunned as she was.

They both seemed to be out of words.

"You can take the car back to your hotel if you want. That way you won't have to take a cab. Then you just have to pick me up tomorrow."

"Tomorrow?" He looked confused.

"Dinner, remember? I said I'd come. You'll make your family happy one last time before heading home and then I'll go practice my flirting skills at another bar." The words fled from her mouth without thought. They had a deal, and she was holding up her end just like he'd held up his.

"You sure?"

The question held so many possibilities, but she couldn't focus on any of them. Her chest tightened in an unfamiliar pain. She forced a bigger smile.

"About what part?" She waved a hand. "It doesn't matter. Yes, I'm sure to all of it. I think I owe you more than you owe me. Your lessons in being a social butterfly are amazing. Before I know it, I'll be the life of the party."

He seemed stiff and awkward, which for Lucas looked strange. "Okay. I'll call you tomorrow and let you know what time I'll pick you up. You sure you won't need your car?"

He spoke while he gathered his clothes from the floor. Felicity felt exposed lying there in a wrinkled skirt and nothing else, so she pulled her tank over her head. "I'll probably just hang out on the beach for a while tomorrow. I can walk from here."

He headed to the door and paused before opening it. She thought for sure he was going to turn and say something, anything, and the urge to tell him to stay burned in her throat, but she remained quiet as he walked out.

Felicity closed the door and slid the lock before leaning her forehead against the wood. She thumped her head against the door as if that had a shot at beating some sense into her.

Pushing away from her spot, she peeled off her clothes and went to the bathroom to shower. Disappointment and longing weighed her down, but she couldn't explain why.

Every time she closed her eyes under the warm spray of the water, she saw Lucas's eyes, warm and friendly and inviting. Everything she was supposed to be.

Then she remembered that he saw her as a project. Something to fix on his short vacation from his real life, a nice diversion from his ex-girl-friend. Becky had been right. Lucas would get bored with her, just like every other guy she'd ever tried to date. She thought she could accept his friendship the same way she had with Layla and Charlie, but now she had her doubts.

Sex with him had been amazing. She could've continued with a friendship after the first time; they had both been scratching an itch while under the influence. Even though that had been different, she knew she'd be able to ignore it.

She'd believed it wouldn't be a problem. She

even thought they could get together when she moved back to Chicago after graduation because things were easy with him. He didn't make her feel like she needed to censor herself, other than when they were in fake relationship mode, and even then, she chose to limit what she said and how she said it. He just let her be.

But tonight shifted everything in her. They had only met three days ago, but it felt so much longer.

The shower hadn't relaxed her the way she'd hoped. Restlessness coursed through her, and the sensation was odd. She didn't like it. For the first time in her life she felt like she couldn't focus. Her brain flitted around and it unnerved her.

She grabbed her e-reader, determined to focus on the story, but less than a paragraph in, she knew that wouldn't work either. Her mind filled with images of Lucas running his large hands over her body, grabbing her, and pulling her to him.

"Ugh." She tossed the reader aside and grabbed her phone. Charlie was always up late. She would tell Felicity what was wrong with her. Charlie didn't sugarcoat anything.

"Hey, Felicity. How's vacation?"

"It's okay, I guess."

"Okay? Why aren't you out getting drunk and partying and getting laid?"

Felicity huffed out a breath. "Layla's stuck in Atlanta, didn't you hear? I'm alone. Kind of."

"Ooo...*kind of* sounds interesting."

"I met this guy on the plane. Lucas." She

paused, not sure what exactly to tell Charlie about how her relationship developed with Lucas. Relationship? Three days and they had a relationship?

"Hello? Did I lose you? Tell me about Lucas. Is he hot?"

"Yeah." She sighed. "He asked me to pretend to be his girlfriend for his brother's wedding." Felicity curled up in the bed under the covers and told Charlie about her three days with Lucas. For a change, Charlie didn't interrupt to call her an idiot once.

"Go you," Charlie said when Felicity finally finished.

"I don't know what's wrong with me. He taught me how to flirt, Charlie. And let me tell you, he did a much better job than you did. But I'm sitting here now and I can't think straight. My brain is bouncing everywhere."

"Oh crap, hon. You're falling for him."

"What? No, I'm not."

"When you see him, do butterflies invade your stomach? Do you smile without having to tell yourself you're supposed to? Does he laugh at your nerd jokes?"

Felicity's heart pounded. She swallowed hard.

"I take your lack of protest to mean that I'm right. You may have the IQ of a genius, but you need to learn to just trust me when it comes to people." She paused and her voice became quiet. "Is it mutual?"

"How the hell should I know?" Felicity squeaked. "I can't read people. You should've come with me. If you were here, you'd be able to tell me."

"Take a deep breath." Charlie waited.

"I don't think I want to fall for him, Charlie. You know how that works for me." She twisted the corner of the blanket in her hand. "I like him. It's like being with you and Layla. I'm not on guard with him."

"That's good. That's the way it's supposed to be."

"But he's a fixer. He's in this because he agreed to fix me. I'm not totally fixable."

"Did he tell you this? Because I might have to fly down there to kick his ass."

"No, I heard his ex-girlfriend say it. But I've watched him for days. He really is a fixer. Everyone comes to him with their problems and he fixes them. Plus, he said he's on a moratorium from women. No dating."

"Why?"

"Why what?"

"Why is he not dating?"

"I don't know."

"Jeez, you really do need me. No guy says that without expecting to answer some questions. You should've asked. Maybe he just said that because he wanted to have an out in case you turned out to be crazy. He could claim that he's taking a break from dating, and he wouldn't have to hurt your feelings." Another pause. "But, if he's laughing at your jokes, he must like you."

"Not funny."

"Of course I am. That's why you keep me

around. Seriously, though, ask him. Be bold. You can do it. See what he says and go from there."

They said their good-byes. Although she felt lighter after talking to Charlie, Felicity was still confused. She only had another day until Lucas left. She couldn't drill him over dinner with his family, especially if Becky was in attendance.

She sent Lucas a text. **You awake?**

Yep.

Why are you on a dating moratorium?

Because I have some stuff to think about. Get my head on straight.

So it was a real moratorium. Or he thought she still had the potential for crazy. Either way was indicative of his need for distance from her.

What are you doing? Reading your porn books?

She smiled in spite of herself. **Maybe.**

I shouldn't have asked. I don't need that image in my head when I'm trying to fall asleep. I'll talk to you tomorrow. Sleep well.

So he didn't want to talk. She had no way of knowing how to navigate this mess, so she curled up and sought sleep. When she closed her eyes, she dreamed of Lucas wanting her to stop pretending.

CHAPTER TEN

*L*ucas fielded a handful of questions from his mother and sister before telling Felicity what time he'd pick her up for dinner. Both Mom and Mia were getting suspicious about his relationship with Felicity. Telling them that she was staying here for the remainder of the week without him had been a mistake. He'd almost told them the truth, but then he thought about Felicity.

If he came clean about their phony relationship, he would have no reason for her to join them for dinner. And he really wanted to have one last night with her, even if her mind was on picking up other men. All day, he'd thought about how to approach the topic of her giving them a chance at a relationship. She'd said her past relationships hadn't worked basically because she was weird.

He liked her weirdness. It was a long shot, and he knew it. He was going back to Chicago to work, and she was returning to Harvard. But after graduation, she was coming home to Chicago. They could do the long-distance thing for a couple of months. He had sick days he could use to take long weekends to visit her. And he had a free plane ticket from his trip down here. It could work.

If she wanted it to.

His phone rang, and he answered without looking, hoping it was Felicity.

"Okay, I think I have it." Mia again.

"Have what, Mia?"

"She's a hooker, right?"

His brain took a minute to figure out where Mia was going with this. When it hit him, he burst out laughing. Felicity, a hooker?

"I won't tell Mom. Tell me the truth."

"Felicity is not a hooker." He shrugged his shirt on and straightened it. The best thing about having a wedding and all these family obligations at a tourist resort was that at least he didn't have to dress up.

"But I know something's up. Just spill it."

"Mia, leave Felicity alone. I like her. A lot."

"I know that, dummy. But she's not your usual type."

"I have a type?"

Her groan came across the line, and he could almost hear her eyes rolling back in her head.

"You like damaged damsels in distress."

"What?"

Another suffering sigh. "Come on, Lucas. You know, for such a smart guy, you sure are dense sometimes. Look at your girlfriends: Carrie, Lisa,

Megan...and who was that one with the wild hair? The one who came to the house..."

"Denise."

"Yeah, her. They all were messed up. Addictions, neediness, self-destructive behavior. How can you not see that?"

He sat on the bed and felt his shoulders sag. When Becky had accused him of just this, he'd broken up with her, telling her that she was controlling and manipulative. She was the reason for his moratorium on women. He'd wanted to believe that she was wrong, but now Mia saw the same thing.

What the hell was wrong with him?

"I like her too."

Mia's words broke through his concentration. "Huh?"

"Felicity. I like her too. Try not to screw it up." Mia hung up without another word.

His fear was that he already somehow managed to do just that.

HOURS LATER, FELICITY SAT BY HIS SIDE AT A TABLE with his family like she belonged there. Mia had her laughing about something that happened at school, and Lucas's chest loosened the tension it had been holding on to. Mia had said nothing else to him about Felicity, and he hoped she wouldn't mention their conversation to Felicity.

He was still sorting out how to talk to her, to see if they had a chance as dinner wrapped up.

His parents had already taken care of the bill and left. The newlyweds had been so close to getting naked at the table that Mom had shooed them off first. Only half the bridal party remained, and unfortunately, Becky was one of them.

As chairs emptied, she scooted closer to sit beside him. Felicity was still engrossed in her conversation with Mia. Now, they were talking about perfume and how people smell, and even if he wanted to follow the conversation, he couldn't. Felicity's hand landed on his leg, palm up. He interlaced his fingers with hers just as Becky bumped his shoulder.

"About the other night at the wedding," she started, her voice so low that he needed to lean closer. "I don't know what Felicity thought I was doing. *I* didn't know what I was doing." She paused and closed her eyes for a second. "That's not true. I thought we might get back together at the wedding. I thought she was some floozy you picked up to be able to keep distance from me."

His spine stiffened, and he glanced out of the corner of his eye to see if Felicity showed any reaction. Her thumb stroked the back of his hand. The slight movement soothed him. Becky's comments bothered him on many levels. First, because there was truth to them. He was guilty of exactly what Becky accused. But never had he thought Felicity to be anything other than brilliant and funny.

He was really an ass to use her the way he had.

Becky patted his other leg. "I just wanted to

apologize. I wish you both the best." Then she stood and walked away.

Lucas stared after her for a moment. The conversation to his left quieted, and he turned to Mia and Felicity. Felicity looked around him, saw that Becky had left, and slid her hand from his grasp. Again, the idea struck him that she thought she was socially inept, but she'd instinctively known what he needed in that moment.

That wasn't something he'd taught her to get through cocktail hour.

Mia suddenly excused herself, and Lucas realized that he and Felicity were alone at the table. Everyone had gone in their own directions. She smiled warmly at him. "That went well."

"You're a natural."

A small laugh puffed through her lips. "When are you leaving tomorrow?"

"Late morning."

"Oh."

"Thank you for everything. All I expected from this weekend was for you to make it bearable for me. You were so much more. I planned to apologize for using you, but I have no regrets. I hope you don't either."

"Regrets?" Her forehead wrinkled like she was faced with a puzzle. "I owe you a thank-you. You taught me so much. I've had a great time, and I never thought that was possible without Layla and Charlie."

He tossed his napkin on the table. "Do you want to go for a walk or..."

"You can go. You've taught me well. Time to

remove the training wheels. I think I'll take my chances at the bar over there. Besides, you probably have to get ready for your plane ride tomorrow."

His stomach twisted at the thought of the plane again. Especially knowing she wouldn't be there to hold his hand and talk him through. "I don't suppose you want to take that plane ride with me. I could use a partner to keep me sane."

She lifted a shoulder. "Sorry. My plane doesn't leave until Saturday." She pushed away from the table. "Do I owe you anything for dinner?"

He stood beside her, searching for the words that might keep her by his side. None came. "My parents took care of it."

"Well, tell them thank you." She rose on tiptoe and kissed his cheek at the same moment he turned his head to kiss hers.

Their lips collided in a clumsy mess, more awkward than any interaction they'd shared. But even in the accidental kiss, he felt her soften against him, and he wanted more.

She jerked her head back. "Sorry. I didn't mean—"

Surely if she wanted the same, she wouldn't have pulled away. She'd been aggressive in bed. Felicity was the kind of woman who took what she wanted. He smiled at her, accepting defeat. "No problem. Have a good time on the rest of your vacation. Give me a call if you need anything."

"You too." She grabbed her purse and walked through the crowd toward the bar.

Lucas left the restaurant and tried to figure out where he'd gone wrong.

FELICITY FORCED HER FEET FORWARD EVEN THOUGH her body wanted to stay near Lucas. Her body craved his touch, even after the smashed kiss. She licked her lips and tasted him. At the bar, she found a free stool and ordered a beer. While waiting for the drink, she spun her chair, much like she had when Lucas had given her a lesson in flirting.

The bartender placed the bottle near her elbow, and as she picked it up, she made accidental eye contact with a guy three seats down. He had dark hair and a day's worth of scruff on his jaw. She smiled and then looked away.

The other faces at the bar blurred together, and she landed back on the guy three seats down. When their eyes met this time, he too smiled. Felicity took a drink from her bottle, and the guy walked over to her.

"Hi, I'm Nick. Can I join you?"

"I'm Felicity. It doesn't look like there's a free stool here."

"We could grab a table."

She thought for a moment. This was what she'd wanted all along. She'd successfully flirted. A pat on the back was in order, but she didn't feel like celebrating. "Sure," she answered before Nick could change his mind.

She followed him to an empty table and set her beer in front of her. "Here on spring break?"

"Yeah, you?"

"Uh-huh. What school do you go to?"

"Stanford."

And so it started. Felicity was actually at ease with this small talk. She had her arsenal of questions at the ready, but found she didn't need to dig too deep. Nick was an excellent conversationalist who kept things moving.

All she wanted to do, though, was tell Lucas that she'd been successful. Then an idea struck. "Can I take a picture of you? Maybe of us together? I want to send it to a friend."

"Okay." Nick's smile remained genuine as if her request wasn't at all odd.

She pulled out her phone, and he put his arm around her shoulder, bringing his head close to hers. She snapped a quick photo, and he moved away. "Thanks."

She tapped out a quick text to Lucas. **Look. You fixed me. You were right. It wasn't hard at all.** Her finger hovered over the send button. Was this one of those things she would regret because she hadn't thought it through?

"Another beer?" Nick asked, interrupting her debate.

"No, I'm good. Thanks."

She hit send and sipped from her drink. Nick went to the bar. As he walked away, she was suddenly reminded of Lucas all over again. The two men had similar traits: tall, dark hair, talkers. Maybe hooking up with Nick wasn't a good idea.

Her phone vibrated in her hand.

You never needed fixing.

She stared at the words. She'd sent Lucas a joke to make him smile, and he was serious. In her head, she heard his voice say the words. If he really meant that, if she wasn't a project to him...

Nick wound back through the crowd to their table. Felicity jumped off her seat and grabbed her purse. She thought she might escape before Nick arrived, but he moved too fast. "I have to go see my friend."

"Can I have your number? Call you?"

She was already moving away from the table. Over her shoulder, she called, "Uh, yeah, maybe later."

It wasn't until she reached the elevator that she realized her response made no sense, but it didn't matter if Nick thought she was dumb. All she could think about was Lucas.

An entire flight of butterflies swarmed her insides, and she jabbed the button for the elevator. What if she was wrong? What if she was interpreting his words to mean what she wanted instead of his intended meaning? What if she ended up looking like an idiot in front of Lucas?

The doors swooshed open, and she automatically stepped in with three other people, but the last thought had her hesitating before pressing the button for his floor.

She didn't think she could handle Lucas looking at her like she was dumb. Even with all of the mistakes she'd made over the course of the last few days, he'd never once looked at her like she was stupid for not understanding something.

Closing her eyes, she pictured his face. His friendly eyes smiling at her, his gentle hand holding hers. No, even if he thought she was dumb, he wouldn't let her see. She reached around the guy in front of her and pressed the button. The ride was faster than she remembered, and the doors opened again on his floor.

She stepped off, staring at the pattern on the carpet, trying to find the words for when he would answer her knock. A door closing down the hall had her raising her head so she could avoid a collision.

There he was, standing with one hand still on the doorknob. A smile burst on her face, and while she felt a little silly, she couldn't control it. He froze staring at her, and a stab of fear that he was going out smacked her.

Be cool, Felicity. This is Lucas. You know how to talk to him.

"Hey, going somewhere?"

"Uh, yeah."

She stopped her progress toward him.

He stepped forward. "To see you. I was headed down to the bar."

"Oh." The smile that she hadn't realized faded returned to her face. "Then I guess you have a minute." She walked the rest of the way to meet him, but didn't get another word out.

Lucas reached for her, lowering his body to align with hers. His hand cradled her head, fingers tangled in her hair, and kissed her. His lips were warm and insistent, and he licked the seam of her mouth. She opened for him, but he controlled the kiss. Every movement, every angle.

She had no idea how long they stood in the middle of the hallway making out, but she was breathless when he finally pulled away. Her heart raced and blood pounded in her ears. Heat flushed through her body as nerves vibrated with want.

"Glad you came back," he whispered.

"So am I." She stepped closer to him, backing him against the wall. "About this moratorium you have going on..."

"It ended the moment I met you."

"Really? You said you needed a break, and I thought you wanted to keep your distance from me because I was your project, something to fix." She still couldn't quite catch her breath. She was leaning into his long, muscular body, and his strong arms were wrapped around her.

"You asked me for help. I wasn't trying to fix you."

"I'm all those annoying traits I told you about."

"I think I can work with that."

She rubbed her body against his. "I have my hotel room for the rest of the week. Do you need to go back to Chicago tomorrow?"

His hands traveled down her back and grabbed her hips. "It's spring break. I only planned to go back because I had nothing to keep me here."

He hoisted her up so she could wrap her legs

around him. His erection poked her and she moaned. "And now?"

"I have a damn good reason to stay. Will you hold my hand on the plane?"

"Maybe we should ditch the tickets and drive back to Chicago." She kissed his neck and bit down on his earlobe. "We could make many stops along the way."

He turned her toward his door and slid the key card in. "That sounds like a plan."

Don't miss the other novellas in the Hot & Nerdy series: *Her Best Shot* and *Her Perfect Game*. Keep reading for an excerpt from each. If you want to see what happens in Vegas after graduation, sign up for my newsletter for a free epilogue.

If you liked *Her Winning Formula*, be sure to check out Shannyn Schroeder's contemporary romance series, The O'Learys:

More Than This
A Good Time
Something to Prove
Catch Your Breath
Just a Taste
Hold Me Close

After checking into a cheap motel for the night, Layla received a text from Felicity with the resort information. With thoughts of the beach and sexy guys, Layla slept for a few hours, but was woken by dreams of working in an office, shuffling papers, and staring at a computer screen in a cubicle, boring herself to tears. The office had no windows, just rows of partitions, where she could hear, but not see other people clicking on keyboards and answering phones.

She took a quick shower to clear her head and decided to hit the road early. Once in her car, thoughts of the gray, dreary dream haunted her. There was no way her new job would be that boring, right? She would be faced with numbers and problems to solve every day. She drove and tried to think of sunnier subjects.

The tightness in her chest was a telltale sign of an impending anxiety attack. She hadn't had one since just before high school graduation, but she'd never forget the feeling. A tingling itchiness invaded her limbs.

Pulling over to the shoulder of the highway, Layla rolled down her windows to get some semi-fresh air. She closed her eyes and breathed deeply. Freaking out over graduating and starting a new job made no sense. This was part of life. Everyone did it. She shook her head, turned up the radio, and pulled back into traffic.

Growing up was a little scary. But she had this week when she didn't have to think about it. For spring break, she could be a girl without a plan, one who didn't know anxiety.

So much for not knowing anxiety. Layla walked down the busy street in Atlanta looking for the nearest bar. She needed a drink.

After a leisurely drive through the mountains and taking time to enjoy the beauty of rural North Carolina, Layla had been feeling better. Then she had pulled into Atlanta and everything went to hell. Her car just stopped. She probably shouldn't have ignored the clunking while she was in the mountains. She sat at the side of the road waiting for a tow truck for a couple of hours. Not that she didn't have offers, from a variety of good old boys, to take her wherever she wanted to go.

Because it was Saturday afternoon, the mechanic had told her straight-out that nothing would be done on her car until Monday, but he'd promised to call her with a diagnosis before the end of the day. She had barely stopped herself from telling him to just fix it no matter what. Although she didn't like being stranded in Georgia, she wasn't going to pay an exorbitant amount of money out of desperation for her hand-me-down car.

Pulling her backpack higher on her shoulder, she stood still for a moment and allowed her eyes to adjust to the dim interior of the first bar she found. It was a dive, but there was a decent-sized crowd. Unfortunately, it wasn't her kind of crowd. They were mostly men and mostly grubby-looking. Even the younger ones had a roughness about them.

Layla figured it was par for the course. All she wanted to do was drown her sorrows in some beer and then pass out until her car was fixed. Maybe she could salvage part of her break. She shot a text to Felicity to let her know about the car.

After ordering a light beer at the bar, Layla walked around to find a spot to drink alone. In the back, she found a few men playing pool at the two tables. She grabbed a chair and sat with her back to the wall so she could watch the players. No one seemed to take notice of her presence.

Within moments, one player easily stood out as the man to beat. He was tall, over six feet, with long dark hair pulled back into a ponytail. He wore a T-shirt that looked intentionally too tight, showing off defined muscles, as if to say, "Don't fuck with me." He didn't chat with the other player. The only sounds he made were to call his shots. He was smooth and efficient, and fun to watch as he cleared the table.

Especially when he bent over in front of her. Maybe being stuck in Atlanta for the night wouldn't be so bad if all the guys were this nice to look at. With the eight ball sunk, the man stood and collected the money sitting on the edge of the table. The loser walked away, and another guy took his place, putting his twenty on the edge.

This second player was better than the first, but Mr. Nice Ass stayed ahead. After a while, Layla began to wonder if he was just toying with his competition, like a cat playing with its prey. He let the other man sink a few balls and then returned to clear the table. Again, he sank the eight ball and swiped the cash.

The man was a pool hustler.

After the second loser left, the man looked around, his gaze landing on her. His eyes, a gray-green, weren't pretty, but were mesmerizing. Something about the contrast against his olive skin.

He pointed his pool cue at her. "Are you going to sit there staring all night, or are you going to play?"

"Me? I'm not stupid enough to play pool with a hustler. My day's been crappy enough. I don't need to lose anything else."

He stalked closer to her. "I'm not a hustler. Hustlers pretend to be bad and then show their true ability to win big. Make no mistake. I'm always good."

As he spoke, she listened to the cadence of his

voice. He didn't have the accent that the other men had. She couldn't tell where he was from.

"Thanks for the vocabulary lesson. I still have better things to do with twenty bucks than lose it to you, especially since I've only played pool a handful of times."

He took another step closer. Close enough that she could touch him if she wanted, but he kept enough distance so she wasn't crowded. "How about you buy me a beer, and I'll give you a lesson?"

She had nothing else going on, and a game of pool with a sexy stranger might be fun. "You're on. What'll you have?"

He tilted his head toward her bottle. "Whatever you're having is fine."

She grabbed her backpack and went back to the bar to buy a couple more beers. When she returned, he had the balls racked and ready to go. She placed her backpack on her chair and grabbed a cue stick. Layla handed him a bottle and said, "I'm Layla."

He took the bottle from her, allowing his thumb to brush over her fingers. "Thanks, Layla. I'm Phin."

The simple touch sent a jolt of pleasure up her arm and down her center. He took a swig of beer, and she watched his throat work as he swallowed. She licked her lips, and when he reached past her to put his bottle on the table, her mouth went dry. This man was like a walking orgasm. He didn't have to say anything, and she wanted to go for a test run.

"Let's get started." He moved back to the pool table. "Do you want to break, or should I?"

"Go ahead." She stood to the side, gripping her cue stick.

He leaned forward, and the roped muscles of his forearms flexed as he made his shot. He sank a solid-colored ball, but because she was too busy watching him and not the table, she didn't see which one.

"Do you know the rules?"

She nodded. "You sank a solid, so I have stripes. Call what pocket I'm aiming for and get the balls in. Don't sink the eight until the end."

"First rule, watch the table." He followed this with a warm grin that told her he liked to tease.

Two could play at that. He leaned over for his next shot, and she shifted closer to him and leaned on the edge. The muscle in his jaw twitched and he straightened.

He carefully set down his stick and walked behind her. Before she could register what was happening, Phin had picked her up by her hips and a squeal popped from her throat. He set her down a couple of feet back.

When she had her balance, she crossed her arms and looked up at him. "What are you doing?"

He cleared his throat before answering. "You can't lean on the table during another player's shot."

She gave him a wide-eyed look. "How else am I supposed to learn? I paid for a lesson, and if you think that watching you win is going to teach me, you're wrong. I might not look like much, but I'm pretty competitive. You'll beat me, but I'm a quick study."

"I'll keep that in mind. Now stay back." He pointed his stick in her direction. "Seven, side pocket." He tapped the pocket he aimed for as if she couldn't figure it out. The ball thunked in and he continued. "Three, corner pocket."

This time, as he leaned over, Layla strolled to the other side of the table. He didn't move his head, but she felt him staring at her. He struck the cue ball, but it angled and glanced off the three, missing his intended target. "Your shot."

Layla stared at the table, trying to decide what would be her easiest shot, instead of taking another peek at his ass. She walked around the corner to get a full picture of where the balls sat and where they should go. When she returned to Phin's side, she asked, "Fifteen in the corner. That's my best bet, right?"

Charlie walked through her apartment, keenly aware of the quiet. Her roommate Amy usually left the TV or the radio playing. Sometimes both. Charlie glanced to the kitchen counter and saw two wine glasses sitting near the sink.

Oh goody, Amy had her boyfriend over. Again. Charlie was trying not to be a bitch about it, but the man was in their place more than Charlie was, and he wasn't paying for anything. What made it worse was that he'd eat her food, like her favorite yogurt, and then not even have the decency to offer a fake apology.

She yanked her hair free from her ponytail and kicked her shoes off, nudging them close to the door so she could easily find them in the morning. Work had beaten her down tonight. As much as she hated the morning shift at a coffee shop, she could at least understand why people might be rude to her. She tended to land on the far side of testy without her morning dose of caffeine. But at seven in the evening?

Tonight had been one of those nights when she could do nothing right. Even if she thought it had been right, the customers didn't agree. All she wanted was a hot shower and some time to play *The Order of Resskaar*. As she grabbed her pajamas from her room, she heard quiet moans coming from the other side of the wall she shared with Amy.

Good thing Charlie owned an excellent pair of headphones. Her dry spell would make hearing Amy and her boyfriend go at it difficult at best. Charlie didn't like being jealous, but it had been way too long since she'd experienced a screaming orgasm, regardless of what her good friends believed.

Part of that was because Ethan had never hit the mark that some men did. He hadn't been a bad lover, exactly, just not as good as others. She sighed and started the hot water. She needed to flush men from her mind. Only two months remained in the school year, and then she wouldn't be able to hold her secret anymore.

Telling everyone—her mom, Layla, Felicity—that she had dropped out of school would sting a whole lot less if she at least had a plan figured out. Having time to implement that plan would be even better.

After her shower, Charlie went back to her room and tuned out the sounds of the squeaky bed banging against the wall. She booted up her computer and put on her headphones. She hoped

Win was online because she could really use a friend tonight. He'd take her mind off her lame job and whiny customers. And if it was a quiet night, maybe they could sneak away for some private time.

So much for flushing men from her mind.

But Win didn't count. He was a virtual man. Well, she was pretty sure he was a man in the real world too, but she only knew him virtually, as a dwarven mage. And it would stay that way unless she could finally convince him to join her at the convention. They would have so much fun together. Even outside the bedroom.

As the home screen welcomed her, Charlie began to relax. She turned the volume up on her stereo to drown out Amy's noise. She preferred to listen to music while she played and just read the conversation on screen. In her head, the characters had natural voices, and the computerized versions never sounded real enough, so she ignored them.

She shot a message to Win. *You around?*

No one answered, so she wandered through the virtual forest looking for the rest of the members of her guild. At least two others were logged on. As she walked, she noticed that her friends had picked up some treasures while she'd been at work. Looking at the loot, she saw things that they had all agreed were unnecessary for their mission. She sighed. This happened every now and then, especially when new members joined the guild.

She didn't try to restrict membership, but she

had guidelines for what she expected the group to be. They were called The Guardians after all. Stealing from people and taking things they didn't need went against everything they stood for. She searched for the tree that would have the items tied to the boughs out of sight. When she found the bag, she took it with her to the village. Starting at the orphanage, she handed out items that others would use to barter to stay alive.

That's when she ran into Kraven. He was the newest member of the guild, and she suspected he was the one responsible for the bag.

What are you doing? That's my stuff.

I'm spreading the wealth. That's what we do.

Do you know how many people I had to go up against to earn that?

I have no idea. What were you planning to do with it?

Save it to exchange for things we'll need. There are only a few more missions until we reach the final one. We'll need supplies to help Resskaar.

I'm in no hurry to reach the final battle. I told you that when you asked to join my guild.

Your guild? I assumed it was Win's guild. He was the one who invited me.

Win invited you after talking to me.

Figures. I'm out. Kraven snatched the bag from her hand and took off with whatever of his loot remained. He sneered at a few of the villagers, but he knew better than to take what she had just given them.

Confronting Kraven left a bad taste in her mouth. She'd come to the game tonight to find refuge, not a fight. Now, however, a fight might make her feel better. She checked the mission status. The others from her guild had logged off, except Kraven. She was on her own. She marched to the edge of town and took off in a run to find the band of marauders she knew had taken up camp.

The thieves stormed every village they came across until they left nothing but a shell behind. She knew she wouldn't be able to take them all on, but her health was near one hundred percent, so she could handle a couple before retreating.

In the distance, she saw the small campfire. As she neared the edge of the camp, she crept along the tree line. If she could find the right vantage point, she could take out half the group without breaking a sweat. Spotting a low-hanging branch, she jumped and climbed. When she found a good bough, one with enough coverage to hide her but still allow a clean shot with her arrow, she settled in. As she surveyed the group below her, a ping told her one of her guild had just logged on.

Win.

It was silly that her heartbeat quickened at the sight of his name, but every time she saw it, it was like she knew she'd be able to see a good friend.

Hey, gorgeous, where are you? Not in our cave.

She typed back quickly. *In a tree about to cause some trouble. Want to join me?*

On my way.

That was one of the many reasons she loved Win. He didn't ask questions; he just came. She got comfortable on her branch while she waited for him and developed a plan. She knew which men she'd need to take out first, and now that Win would have her back, she could attack and he could swoop in and take their cache.

By the end of her night, she'd at least make a few other people secure, and that might be enough to make up for her evening.

Moments later, she saw the rustle of a bush and knew Win had arrived. He always knew where to find her. She launched her first arrow, nailing one soldier's shoulder. She'd taken out two more before the others realized what was happening. Unfortunately, they figured out quickly where she was and came at her.

She jumped from her branch and led them away from Win's position. Without the rest of their guild, he didn't stand a chance against these monsters. She might be able to outrun them. It seemed like a good plan until one shot a rock and hit her in the head. A breath later they were on her, kicking her and throwing more stones. Her life energy was waning fast. She tried to scramble to her feet, but it was no use. They outnumbered her and had her surrounded.

Suddenly a flash fire burst around her and she sighed. If it had been the enemy, she'd be in flames. This was Win's doing. The group tossed a few more rocks in her direction, but gave up when they realized that it wasn't worth the health points to get past the fire.

Thanks for having my back.

That was a stupid move. You okay?

Been better.

Then the flames died and Win stood there staring at her, a stuffed bag flung over his shoulder. The mission was a success.

Come on. He leaned over to pick her up.

In the quiet of her bedroom, Charlie laughed out loud. Win was a dwarf, a short, round guy about half her height. He was strong, though, and he hefted her and ran back to their cave.

You need to be more careful, Laura.

Win almost never called her by name. It suddenly struck her as weird. She called him Win all the time, but he never called her Laura.

They didn't speak again until they were safe and Win healed her. He was always doing that, taking care of her. Not that she didn't do her share of saving his ass, but he was a healer and she was a warrior. They made a hell of a team.

When she had regained her strength, she sat in front of the fire Win had built for them.

Have you thought about coming to the con next week?

I told you, I don't know if I can.

If it's money, you can crash in my room. All you need is registration.

We'll see.

She winked at him. *It'll be fun.* Then she curled up to sleep. Win lay beside her and everything in her calmed.

If only she had that in real life.

Hot & Nerdy

Her Best Shot

Her Perfect Game

Her Winning Formula

His Work of Art

His New Jam

His Dream Role

O'Learys

More Than This

A Good Time

Something to Prove

Catch Your Breath

Just a Taste

Hold Me Close

For Your Love

Under Your Skin

In Your Arms

Through Your Eyes

From Your Heart

Stand Alones

Between Love and Loyalty

Meeting His Match

<u>Daring Divorcees Series</u>

One Night with a Millionaire

My Best Friend's Ex

My Forever Plus-One

www.ingramcontent.com/pod-product-compliance
Lightning Source LLC
Chambersburg PA
CBHW050539190726
48284CB00003B/1135